"I'm not the bad guy here."

Lexie laughed incredulously. "You're saying I am?"

"You don't take your responsibilities seriously," Rafe explained. "Absentmindedness is no excuse for failing to file a tax return."

"Humph." She stood in an indignant tinkling of bells, swished away a few paces before she spun around in a whirl of skirt. "You're just like my family. Oh, that scatterbrained Lexie— she can't handle her finances, she can't take care of herself, much less a baby. Maybe I have different priorities. Maybe money and... and receipts aren't the most important things in life. Maybe people are."

"That's what I'm saying. People need hospitals and schools and roads—" His hands rested on the keyboard as he stared at her. "What baby?"

Dear Reader,

Life, it seems to me, is largely a matter of timing. What if you meet your soul mate but one or both of you aren't ready to settle down? Would you say goodbye and hope you'll find someone else someday who'll be as perfect for you? Or would you grab him and never let him go, regardless of the monkey wrench it throws in your life's plans?

When to have children is another major life decision that depends so much on "being ready." What if one person wants a baby and the other doesn't—or at least doesn't yet? Is that a deal breaker?

I wasn't interested in marriage and children until I was close to thirty years old. But when I was finally ready to settle down, my husband came along. It felt as if I'd been waiting, without knowing it, just for him.

I've had fun playing around with questions of timing in *Two Against the Odds*. Life doesn't flow quite as smoothly for my hero and heroine as it did for me and my hubby. Add to that the fact that Lexie Thatcher is twelve years older than Rafe Ellersley and the question of babies and timing takes on a new urgency.

Two Against the Odds is the third book in the Summerside Stories trilogy. Lexie's parents, Hetty and Steve, who have been having their own trials throughout these stories, finally find the key to their own happiness.

I love to hear from readers.
You can email me at www.joankilby.com or write to me
c/o Harlequin Enterprises Limited,
225 Duncan Mill Road, Don Mills,
Ontario, Canada
M3B 3K9.

Joan Kilby

Two Against the Odds

Joan Kilby

Harlequin®

TORONTO NEW YORK LONDON
AMSTERDAM PARIS SYDNEY HAMBURG
STOCKHOLM ATHENS TOKYO MILAN MADRID
PRAGUE WARSAW BUDAPEST AUCKLAND

Recycling programs
for this product may
not exist in your area.

ISBN-13: 978-0-373-71693-7

TWO AGAINST THE ODDS

Copyright © 2011 by Joan Kilby

This edition published by arrangement with Harlequin Books S.A.

For questions and comments about the quality of this book
please contact us at Customer_eCare@Harlequin.ca.

www.eHarlequin.com

Printed in U.S.A.

ABOUT THE AUTHOR

Joan Kilby enjoys drawing and painting as a hobby. However, between her writing, her husband and three almost-grown children, going to the gym, cooking and walking her dog, Toby, she doesn't have a lot of spare time to indulge her other interests. Instead, she lives vicariously through characters like the heroine of *Two Against the Odds,* artist Lexie Thatcher. Joan also loves art galleries and every year makes a point of going to see the exhibition of the Archibald Prize finalists.

Books by Joan Kilby

HARLEQUIN SUPERROMANCE

*Summerside Stories

CHAPTER ONE

RAFE ELLERSLEY WAS kind of like Snoopy—always daydreaming about things he'd rather be doing, such as going fishing. Unlike Snoopy, he didn't have a doghouse to lie atop, just a cramped cubicle at the Australian tax office.

"I need a volunteer for an audit in Summerside." Larry Kiefer, balding and forty, with a slight gut, walked among the cubicles filled with tax accountants at the Australian tax office. "Who's interested?"

Rafe shot to his feet. "I'll do it." He'd have gone anywhere just to get out of the office, but Summerside was ace. A small bayside village southeast of Melbourne, it was prime red snapper territory.

Sunshine, blue sky and salt water. Oh, yeah.

Larry pretended not to see him. "Anyone? This lady—" He consulted a file folder in his hand. "Lexie Thatcher is a portrait artist. She hasn't filed a return in four years."

Rafe cleared his throat. "Larry, I said I'd do it."

His colleagues nearby glanced at him, then at Larry. They didn't say a word. It was unwritten code that if someone put up their hand for a case, everyone else would bow out. One by one, they bent their heads and went back to work.

Rafe remained standing. But not quite as tall as before.

His previous audit hadn't gone so well....

Larry made a sour face and shook his head. He was the boss. He could simply assign the case to whomever he chose. But Rafe knew he tried to hand the out-of-town files to whomever was interested.

He walked slowly over to Rafe's cubicle, gave a last glance around then, when no one looked up, he said to Rafe, "What makes you think you're the right guy for this job?"

"I want to make up for last time." Rafe fumbled for an antacid and popped it in his mouth. His five-year plan depended on keeping his position and if that meant pretending to be sorry for what he'd done, so be it. The great fishing would be a bonus.

Larry checked out Rafe's cubicle. The partition walls were papered with photos of boats, his dog Murphy and Far Side cartoons he'd clipped out of the newspaper.

"Your last audit, Mrs. Caporetto, was working under the table *and* collecting welfare," Larry reminded him. "She wasn't paying a cent of tax on her waitressing income. Do you think that's fair to other taxpayers?"

"She was supporting her son who had cancer, plus his three children," Rafe said, arguing anyway, to defend Mrs. Caporetto, and himself. "Like I told you, the dole wasn't enough money for them all to live on. Not with the meds her son needed."

"We've been through this. That's not our problem," Larry said wearily. "You deliberately turned a blind eye and didn't impose penalties when they were clearly called for. It's not your job to make sure auditees pay the *least* amount of taxes possible. You do know that, don't you?"

Rafe nodded. He picked up a pen, clicking it in and out. Across the way, his buddy Chris Talbot faced his computer screen, heavy blond hair falling over his glasses, and pretended not to be listening.

"Not paying taxes is like stealing from the government," Larry went on. "You're not some Robin Hood."

Rafe bit his lip.

"It's essential for tax auditors to…?" Larry prompted, waiting for Rafe to complete the sentence.

"Maintain an independent state of mind," Rafe intoned. It was the mantra of the tax office, ingrained in all tax auditors from day one.

Larry cocked his egg-shaped head to glance at Rafe's photos of fishing boats. "Did you ever think maybe you're not cut out to be an accountant?"

"I'm cut out for it." Rafe chewed the softening remains of the antacid tablet. "I can do it."

One more year and he would have saved enough

money to put a down payment on a charter fishing boat. His dream was to take groups out on the weekend. Hell, why stop at the weekend? Someday he wanted to make fishing charters his livelihood.

If he could hang on to this job until then.

Lose it, and he wouldn't easily find another that paid this well. Especially if he got fired.

"You could be one of the best accountants I've got," Larry said. "Question is, do you have the balls to be that guy?"

Rafe swallowed and nodded again. "You can count on me."

"This woman…" Larry waved the file folder. "Hasn't responded to letters, emails or phone calls. She's going to be a tough nut to crack." He dropped the file on Rafe's desk. "Screw this one up and…" He walked away, leaving the rest hanging.

Rafe swallowed. He didn't need Larry to spell things out to know the consequences would be dire.

LEXIE THATCHER WAS a crystal lying on the sandy bottom of a quiet pond. Calm and peaceful. She was as smooth and round as a washed pebble but perfectly clear. Crystal clear. Sunlight filtering through the water filled her with a pure white light.

Thoughts crept in like dark tendrils of water weeds—her stalled portrait of Sienna, her parents' disintegrating marriage, the letter from the tax office… Gently she pushed each thought away.

Calm. Peace. Light.

Sienna's portrait was missing a crucial element. What was it? Why was she blocked? The deadline was approaching.

Thirty-eight years old last week.

Time was ticking.

Don't think. Empty the mind. Slow the breathing.

Light. Peace. Calm.

Peace. Calm—

Ding-dong.

Lexie crashed to earth with a jerk. Now she felt the rough nap of the carpet beneath her palms, the weight of her legs, her yoga top bunched at her waist. The noisy thoughts came awake in her head, all clamoring for attention at once, like chattering monkeys.

The bell rang again. Ding-dong.

With a sigh she dragged herself upright and padded barefoot to the front door, pushing a hand through her long blond curls, straightening her filmy cotton skirt. Three tiny bells around her right ankle tinkled with each step.

She hoped it was Andrew, the sweet little boy from next door, come to fetch the ball he was forever accidentally throwing over the fence. She loved his adorable freckled face and big green eyes. *Lexie, may I get my ball?*

She opened the door, her gaze pitched to knee level. "Hey, Andrew—"

Not a four-year-old boy with curly red hair.

Charcoal-gray pant legs with a razor-sharp crease and black crocodile-skin shoes. Her gaze skimmed up the long lean figure in the well-cut suit with the white shirt open at the neck. A ripe mouth framed by dark stubble and dark eyes topped by thick black eyebrows. His hair was pushed back showing a strong widow's peak and he had a dark mole high on his right cheek.

He was sexy. And young.

A buzz of awareness hummed through her despite the fact that she had to be at least ten years older than he was. "What can I do for you?"

"Rafe Ellersley." He produced a business card and held it up for her to see. "Australian Taxation Office."

She slammed the door in his face.

She stood there, listening to her heart gallop, knowing he hadn't moved from her welcome mat. Yes, very mature.

Ding-dong.

Lexie put her hand on the knob. Sucking in a breath, she opened the door again. "Sorry. That was dumb."

"I'm used to it." His gaze started to drift down her formfitting sleeveless top then flicked back to her eyes. "I normally don't just show up on people's doorsteps. But when people don't respond to letters or phone calls, a personal visit is the next step."

There *had* been letters, which she'd set aside to deal with later. And then there were the phone messages which she'd ignored because she'd been painting and didn't want to be disturbed. Then when she'd gotten blocked she'd decided their negative energy was her problem and, whoops, they were accidentally-on-purpose deleted. And now her bad habit of procrastination had come around to bite her on the butt.

She breathed deep into her belly to stem her rising panic. "I've been very busy with my work. Is there a problem?"

Rafe set his briefcase on the mat at his feet. "You're being audited."

Her stomach tightened, trapping her breath. "Audited?"

"Yes. I'm here to go over your accounts with you and assess taxes owed for the period of delinquency." He glanced over her shoulder into the small foyer. "Is this a good time?"

"No." Her house was a mess, her work in limbo, her life in chaos. "I'm busy, very busy. I must get back to what I was doing."

Lying on the floor pretending to be a crystal. It was vital to her creativity but hard to explain to a sexy young man in a suit. She started to close the door.

Quick as a wink he wedged a polished shoe

between the door and the jamb. "I understand you're an artist."

"Y-yes," she said warily. She could imagine what tax accountants thought of artists—about as useful to society as bicycles were to fish. "I'm working on a portrait for the Archibald Prize."

"I'll try not to take up too much of your time. May I come in?"

"As I said, I'm busy. I'll file my tax return soon. Promise. On my honor and all that." She gave the door another shove.

His foot didn't budge. With his leg braced, his thigh muscle was outlined against his pant leg. "Then I'll come back later. What time do you finish for the day?"

"I work all hours. Right through the night sometimes, when things are flowing."

In reality, she hadn't done any work on Sienna's portrait for weeks but he didn't need to know that. She hadn't been completely idle, having whipped off a couple of small seascapes of Summerside Bay for the tourist trade. She just hadn't done anything important.

"I'll come back tomorrow," he said.

"I'll be busy then, too!"

Again she pushed on the door to no avail. No doubt the Australian Taxation Office issued steel-reinforced shoes for cases like hers.

Apparently the agents were reinforced with steel,

too. His black eyes glinted; his smile was grim. "Ms. Thatcher, you haven't filed a tax return in four years. I will come back every day. I will camp on your doorstep if necessary, until you make the time to go through your accounts. Whether it takes weeks or months is of no difference to me. I have a job to do and I will do it." He let his words sink in before he added almost casually, "If you don't comply, I have the authority to call in the Federal Police."

A flutter of panic made her reconsider the situation. But she hadn't done anything wrong. True, she hadn't filed her taxes but then again, she didn't think she'd made enough money to pay tax. This was all a misunderstanding that would be cleared up quickly once he'd had a look at her accounts.

"Okay," she capitulated, opening the door wider. "Come in. Let's get this over with. Shoes off, please. I have a friend with a baby who's still crawling."

Color tinged his cheeks as he bent to remove his croc-skin loafers. Avoiding her gaze, he placed the shoes neatly beside her sandals, making them look tiny by comparison. Then she saw the reason for his embarrassment. His fourth toe poked through a hole in the left sock.

Suddenly Rafe Ellersley seemed less daunting, more human. She would have preferred to see him as the enemy.

Lexie led him into the sunny living room. Visible through the big window was the backyard containing a trampoline, her detached studio and, in the corner, a koi pond beneath a red-flowering camellia tree. She moved some art books off an armchair. "Have a seat."

He lowered himself onto faded chintz covered in overblown pink roses, like Ferdinand the Bull in a field of flowers. Lexie sat opposite on the matching couch beneath the window, squished in between her sleeping Burmese cats, Yin and Yang. She tucked her legs up cross-legged and pulled down her full skirt.

"Why am I being audited?" she asked. "Is it random or are you guys targeting starving artists this year?"

"The tax office is focusing on small businesses," he explained with a shrug. "This is an election year. The government wants to be seen to be doing its job."

"But why me?" Lexie asked. "I'm a small fish."

"Small fish, big fish, they all get caught eventually. As I said, you haven't filed a tax return for the past four years." He whipped out a small notebook and consulted it. "Yet last financial year you sold two paintings to an American tourist for forty thousand dollars."

"Oh, right." Lexie pressed paint-stained fingers to her mouth. They'd been her best sales to date. How could she have forgotten them? "I meant to declare them, honest." She paused. "Er, how did you find out?"

"The man hung them in his office and declared them as a tax deduction. The American Internal Revenue Service, doing a random check, cross-referenced with our tax department. And here we are."

"I don't have any of that money left," she said. "It's gone. On rent, clothes, food…" Trivial things like that.

"Why didn't you declare it?"

Procrastination again. "I was planning to average my income over five years."

"Yet you didn't do that, either."

Lexie fidgeted, disturbing Yin, who looked up through green slits of eyes and twitched her creamy tail. Lexie stroked her, soothing her back to purring slumber. "I missed the cutoff date."

"You had seven months from the sale of the painting in which to file." Rafe Ellersley consulted his notebook again. "I understand you were an art teacher at Summerside Primary School until five years ago. Presumably you know how to file an income tax statement."

"As a teacher with a fixed income, preparing a statement was easy. Since I quit my regular job I haven't figured out all the ins and outs of what I need to do as a self-employed artist."

"So you've simply ignored the problem, hoping it will go away." Rafe wrote a few lines in his notebook.

"In a nutshell." She glanced out the window,

calculating the angle of the light slanting through the trees onto her detached studio. She'd hoped to have meditated her way into a creative state and be working by now. Instead, she was stuck here, talking to a tax agent. "How much time will the audit take?"

"That depends," he said. "If your records are in order and easily accessible it could take only a few days."

"Records?" Her fingers pleated the soft fabric of her skirt. She hadn't been able to find her "filing system" for over a month.

"Tax receipts. As in, when you purchase paints and canvases you keep a receipt." His dark eyes bored into her. "You do keep your receipts, don't you?"

"Of course. I save everything in big manila envelopes."

"I'd like you to get them for me, please. Everything for the past five years. Plus bank statements, utility bills, home and contents insurance, et cetera."

"I would but there's a small problem. I put the envelopes away for safekeeping and now I can't find them." When his black eyebrows pulled together, she added quickly, "Oh, don't worry. I never throw anything away." As anyone could guess just by looking at her house.

"What have you been doing with your receipts since then?" he asked.

"They're around," she said vaguely. Tossed in a

drawer, tucked inside a novel as a bookmark, stuffed into a shoe box.

"You'll need to locate them and the envelopes, of course." He glanced about the room. "Where can I set up my laptop? Is there a table or desk I can use as a workspace?"

"Um…" The coffee table, an old trunk she'd painted white, was covered in assorted debris—a used teacup, her sketch pad and box of charcoal and cat toys. The side table at his elbow was obscured by seashells and pretty stones she'd found on the beach. The dining table was strewn with magazines, newspapers and junk mail. And a framed seascape ready to be delivered to the local Manyung Gallery, where she sold works on commission.

"I guess the dining table." She got up and placed the painting on the floor, leaning it against the wall.

Rafe set his briefcase on the table in the space cleared and removed a laptop. Lexie moved around him, gathering the newspapers and magazines. She was aware of how tall he was, at least a head higher than her. And he smelled good, spicy and warm. He was emitting enough pheromones to set her blood humming again.

"Perhaps you have a computer spreadsheet detailing items purchased and the dates?" he asked. "I'd still need the receipts, of course, for verification."

"No spreadsheet," Lexie said. "My sister, Renita,

is a loans officer at the bank. She tried to organize a bookkeeping system for me but I couldn't be bothered filling in all those columns."

He turned his incredulous gaze on her. "Did you read the letter my boss sent you a month ago? Or any of his emails?"

Shaking her head, she took a step back. Pheromones or no, she didn't like an inquisition.

"Did you listen to the messages on your answering machine, at least?"

She rubbed at a spot of Crimson Lake paint on her knuckle. "I did. But when I'm working I tend to tune things out."

"Tune out?" It all seemed too much for Rafe. With a grimace, he pressed a hand to his abdomen.

"Is your stomach bothering you?"

"It'll pass." His voice was tight, his shoulders slightly hunched.

"Is it an ulcer? My uncle had an ulcer."

"I'm fine." He lowered himself onto the chair in front of his laptop, the lines of his face pulled taut.

"I'll make you a cup of peppermint tea." Before he could object she strode out of the dining room into the adjacent kitchen. She filled the kettle at the sink. Crystals hanging in the window cast rainbows over her arms. People sometimes got exasperated with her for being scatterbrained, but she didn't think she'd ever actually made anyone physically ill before.

"My stomach would feel better if you got me your records," he called.

"I'm working on that." While the water heated she looked in the cupboard beneath the telephone where she stored cookbooks. Not surprisingly, there weren't a dozen large envelopes stuffed with receipts and tax invoices. Where had she put those things?

Ah, but here was a receipt for mat board that she'd bought last week. It was tucked inside the address book. Of course. Because she'd rung the gallery right after buying the materials for framing.

Sitting on the tiled floor, she pulled out cookbooks and riffled through the pages. She found a few grocery store receipts itemizing pitifully meager provisions.

"Can I claim food?" she yelled to the other room.

"No, it's not a deductible business expense." Already he sounded long-suffering and he'd been here less than an hour.

She was putting back her mother's copy of *Joy of Cooking,* which she'd borrowed to make quince preserves, when an old photograph fell out of the pages. With paint-stained fingers she slanted it toward the light.

She, her brother, Jack, and sister, Renita, were playing on the front lawn of the dairy farm where they'd grown up. She couldn't have been more than six years old. Jack would have been about four and

Renita just a toddler. Lexie smiled, her eyes misting. They'd had good times as kids.

Now Jack was getting married again and Renita, too. Lexie was the only one of her siblings who hadn't found a life partner. She'd never had the kids she longed for, either. A sharp pang for the baby she'd lost made her press a hand to her chest. She counted back the years.

Her boy would have been twenty-one years old now.

"The kettle is boiling," Rafe said, right behind her.

Lexie tucked the photograph back in the cookbook and, rising, placed the mat board receipt in his open palm. "It's a start."

He stared at the crumpled slip of paper. Resignation washed over his face and his mouth firmed. He unbuttoned his sleeves and rolled them up over his forearms. "We've got a lot of work to do."

"You have no idea," Lexie murmured.

RAFE TOOK a sip of peppermint tea and tried not to grimace. He would give his right arm for a strong cup of espresso—even if it did aggravate his gut. Carefully he set the delicate china teacup with the hand-painted roses in its saucer.

With Lexie's records this disorganized he bet she had other undeclared painting sales. How was she going to pay her taxes? Anyone could see she had no money.

Not his problem. His job was to do the audit and get the hell out of Summerside.

Hopefully after he'd had a chance to sample the fishing.

Seated at the dining table, he went about setting up a spreadsheet for Lexie's tax records. So far she'd managed to find a dozen receipts, gleaned from strange hiding places. The teapot had yielded a receipt for scented tea candles—naturally. Apparently Lexie sometimes meditated by candlelight to enhance her creativity. Too bad for her, the tax office didn't consider them an allowable expense.

Lexie was moving around the living room, searching in decorative wooden boxes and flipping through the pages of books. Never in his six years of auditing had he come across anyone like her. She'd pick something up, carry it a few steps and put it down in another spot.

Nutbags, these artist types.

"Maybe instead of looking for individual receipts, you should concentrate on finding those envelopes you were telling me about," he said.

"I'm deliberately *not* thinking about them in the hopes it'll pop into my mind where I put them."

Nutbag she might be, but she was easy on the eyes. With her straight back and graceful, sleek limbs she could have been mistaken for a dancer. Long tangled blond hair fell past her shoulder blades. She'd bend to search a low shelf then unfold, flipping that hair back, humming to herself as another book or a picture caught her fancy and she spent a few moments studying it. Completely unselfconscious, she didn't seem to care if he watched her.

Not that he was watching her.

With a frown he dragged his attention back to his woefully sparse spreadsheet, labeling columns across the top.

"Do you mind music while you work?" she said, picking out a CD from the vertical rack.

"Go ahead." He gritted his teeth and braced himself for whale songs or some such New Age thing.

"I think you'll like this. It's Geoffrey Gurrumul Yunupingu." She inserted the CD and a soft haunting voice began to sing in another language.

Yep, just as he'd thought. Rafe tuned out and started tapping in numbers. The sooner he got through this, the sooner he could get down to the pier with his fishing rod.

"Ooh, here's a whole bunch," she said, peering into a carved wooden box. She sauntered over to the table and plunked them in front of him. "Here you go."

Four of the six receipts were useless for tax purposes. He added the other two to his meager pile. "Fourteen down, God knows how many to go."

Lexie slid onto a chair and pulled her legs up

beneath her. "So, Rafe, did you always want to be a tax agent when you grew up?"

"Yes, accountancy fascinated me from an early age."

"Really?" Lexie asked, with a dubious frown.

No. But he had a facility for numbers and after graduating from high school, accounting had seemed like the quickest ticket out of the small country town of Horsham where he'd grown up.

Rafe shrugged. "It's a living."

"It can't be nice going to people's houses and threatening them with the police if they don't hand over their receipts."

Another twinge in his stomach. He clenched his teeth to control the wince. Nobody got it. Sure, it wasn't the most thrilling job but it wasn't fair that people saw him as the bad guy. "I'm here to *help* you. You've gotten yourself in trouble and I'm bailing you out. At taxpayers' expense, I might add."

"So you think you're doing a good thing?"

"Yes, I do." His fingers tapped the keys as he inputted her details at the top of the spreadsheet. "Where would we be without roads, hospitals, schools? *I'm* not the bad guy here."

She laughed incredulously. "You're saying *I* am?"

"You don't take your responsibilities seriously. Absentmindedness is no excuse for failing to file a tax return."

"Humph." She stood up in an indignant tinkling of

bells, swished away a few paces then spun around, her skirt whirling. "You're just like my family. That scatterbrained Lexie—she can't handle her finances, she can't take care of herself, much less a baby. Maybe I have different priorities. Maybe money and…and receipts…aren't the most important things in life. Maybe *people* are."

"That's what I'm saying. People who need hospitals and schools and roads." His hands rested on the keyboard as he stared at her. "What baby?"

"Pardon me?" Her skirts settled, her hands clutching the fabric. Color tinged her cheeks. "I didn't say anything about a baby."

"Yes, you did."

"No, I didn't."

CHAPTER TWO

RAFE STARED after her as she hurried from the room, wondering if he'd imagined her saying that about a baby. There was no evidence of an infant or a husband about the house, at least that he could see at a glance. She'd actually mentioned a friend's toddler, not her own. Maybe she was pregnant and didn't have a partner. Maybe she was worried about her future and wasn't sure what to do.

He shrugged and shook his head. Lexie's baby—real, imagined or pending—was none of his business. Kids. He shuddered.

He could hear her banging pots around in the kitchen and glanced at his watch. It was already past noon. The smell of food emanating from the kitchen was making his stomach rumble.

Lexie returned, carrying a tray loaded with two white-and-blue Chinese soup bowls. Steam rose, spoons clinked gently. "My mother always says that a hungry man is a crabby man."

She set the soup in front of him. Two-minute noodles with a few slices of carrot floating on top. He glanced at her bowl and saw that she'd given him the larger portion. Either she was on a strict diet or she was hurting for money.

"You didn't have to feed me," he said. "I planned to go into the village and find a deli for lunch."

"I was cooking anyway." Picking up her spoon, she concentrated on scooping up the slippery noodles.

This was awkward. Rafe didn't usually dine with clients. That wasn't the way for a tax auditor to "maintain an independent state of mind." On the other hand, two-minute noodles weren't exactly a sumptuous bribe that would turn his head.

Lexie herself was a challenge, though. The sensuous way she moved, her blue cat's eyes, the aura of sexuality that set his nerve endings tingling....

Aura? Had he actually thought that word?

She must really be getting to him. It was ridiculous. She wasn't even his age. He couldn't tell exactly how old she was but she was definitely older.

Picking up his bowl, he moved to the side of the table so he didn't slop soup onto his computer and papers. Keeping his eyes down and not on the woman opposite, he tasted the bland, watery broth. "Mmm, good."

She combed her hands through her hair, pushing it back. Despite the paint stains, she wore a lot of rings. How did she keep them clean? "You should try meditating. It might help your ulcer."

"*If* I had an ulcer, acid-blocking medicine would help it more than New Age rubbish."

"How do you know unless you try it?"

"How do you know I haven't?"

A tiny smile curled her lips as she bent her head to her bowl. Rafe watched her full pink lips purse and her cheeks hollow as she sucked in the long noodles. He *hadn't* tried meditating, of course, but he hated it when people made assumptions about him.

He wasn't some weedy dweeb with ink-stained fingers bent over a ledger. In his heart he was a sea-faring man, hunting schools of plump red snapper. Snapper would have been nice right now.

Setting to with his spoon, he emptied the meager contents of his bowl. Then he pushed it away. "I'd better get on with your taxes."

"Finished already? You're like my father and brother. They inhale food." She reached for his bowl. "Do you want more? I could open another packet."

"No, thanks." He patted his belly. "I couldn't eat another thing. Now, Lexie, I really need those envelopes."

She rose to gather the dishes. "I'll go look in my studio. You have my permission to search the house for them. At this point, your guess is as good as mine."

Rafe glanced around at the cluttered room crammed with pottery, books, paintings, notepads, sketch pads, flowers—including fresh, dried and dead—and all the rest of the flotsam and jetsam. No doubt every room in her house was similarly jam-packed. The thought of plowing through it—and on a curdled stomach—made him wince.

He had to get out of this job before it killed him.

LEXIE PERCHED on a wooden stool and studied the portrait of Sienna from across the room. To hell with looking for the envelopes, she needed to get this painting finished.

The canvas was large, six foot by four, and was executed in her signature style, so highly detailed it looked almost as real as a photograph but with a magical quality. Sienna was posed like Botticelli's Venus, draped in royal-blue cloth to set off her Titian hair, which cascaded over her shoulders in abundant loose curls. Her clear grey-green eyes gazed out above a narrow nose very faintly dusted with freckles.

Lexie was satisfied she'd gotten the face right, was pleased she'd captured an expression of alert curiosity. Every hair was painted with attention to texture and color. Along with the creamy skin of Sienna's shoulder and one exposed breast. Sienna looked… alive.

Yet the painting didn't feel complete. Something was missing, Lexie knew it instinctively. She just couldn't put her finger on what. She'd done six versions and this was the best. If she started mucking about again she might ruin what she'd already done.

She tried instead to concentrate on the theme.

Sienna by the bay. The unseen half seashell. Borne on the waves. Born of the sea...

It was no use. Lexie glanced toward the house, wondering what Rafe was up to. Should she have allowed him to look through her things? He was a stranger, after all. He might be going through her underwear. Wouldn't that be... Exciting.

Stop it. Why was she thinking like that? He was way too young for her, practically a boy in short pants. It must be because she was blocked. She always got antsy under pressure.

Sliding off the stool, she walked over to the tall cupboards at the back of the studio. She flung them open, hoping the tax envelopes would jump out at her. Nothing but painting supplies. Crouching lower, she looked through brushes, turpentine, old palettes, sketchbooks, flattened and twisted tubes of used oil paints.

From the doorway, Rafe cleared his throat. "Excuse me. I need to calculate the percentage of household expenses accounted for by your studio."

Lexie stood up, shutting the cupboard. Rafe had walked across the lawn in his socks and a tuft of grass had caught between his bare toe and the torn sock edge.

"This space is roughly a quarter of the square footage of the house. I paint out here and do my framing," she said, gesturing to the trestle table along the side wall piled with off cuts of mat board and empty frames. "But I also use the house to research things on the internet, read art books and magazines."

"Since those are all deductible I'll adjust the percentage upward." He moved into the studio, glancing at Sienna's portrait. "Is this your Archibald Prize entry?"

"It's supposed to be. I can't seem to finish it."

He walked over to the canvas, peered up at Sienna's face. "It looks finished."

Picking a brush out of the jar of turpentine, Lexie cleaned it on a rag. "Something's missing."

Rafe adopted the classic pose of someone looking at a painting, arm across the waist, the other palm cupping the jaw, the studious frown. His broad shoulders stretched the fabric of his white shirt. Lexie's gaze drifted lower. His cocked hip emphasized his butt muscles and the length of his extended leg.

"It's very romantic," he said.

"Thank you."

"I didn't actually mean that as a compliment."

"Why not?" she asked, frowning. With her brother Jack and Sienna falling in love it had been impossible to paint Sienna without an air of romance.

"It needs something to counteract all the beauty. To raise it above sentimentality."

She tossed the brush onto the table with a clatter. He dared to give her advice? "Sentimental!"

He shrugged. "I'm just saying."

Lexie forced herself to study the painting again.

She worked hard at being objective about her own work and she had a pretty thick skin. But she'd never thought her interpretation of Sienna was sentimental. The very word conjured paint-by-number kits and kitschy paintings of doe-eyed children holding floppy sunflowers.

"The hair, the skin, the robe…all lush. The expression in her eyes is very emotional," Rafe explained.

"I know," she said through gritted teeth. "It's what I was trying to achieve. It's supposed to be emotional."

In a series of sittings spanning several months, she and Sienna had talked about many things. A recurring theme had been Sienna's yearning for another child besides Oliver, her teenage son from her first marriage. Now that Sienna was marrying Lexie's brother, Jack, she probably would have a baby. Naturally, there'd been emotion involved. "There's nothing wrong with portraying feelings."

"I didn't say there was."

"It's not sentimental."

"No need to get defensive. I think it's wonderful. I'm just trying to help."

"It's not your cup of tea, that's all."

"You're wrong. I like it a lot," he insisted. "I just think it needs a contrasting note."

That stopped her dead. He turned to her, one eyebrow lifted. Damn. Her silence was starting to look like agreement. He was cocky enough as it was. She couldn't let him think he'd solved her problem. Not that he had solved it. It was one thing to toss off the phrase "contrasting note" like he knew what he was talking about and quite another to figure out what form the contrast should take.

"It has occurred to me that it needs more interior depth," Lexie mused aloud, trying to baffle him with bullshit. "Perhaps a smidgeon more archetypal mystery in her smile. The goddess within, juxtaposed with the beast, as manifested by the exposed breast."

Rafe seemed skeptical at this display of gobbledygook. He studied her a moment then finally laughed.

Lexie lifted her chin, holding his gaze rather than admit she was full of it. Damn. He'd seen right through her.

His laughter faded, his amusement replaced by something intent, almost…hungry. Lexie felt herself growing warm, her breathing shallow.

What was happening here?

Rafe blinked. "I've got to get back to number crunching. I, uh…" He shook his head. "What did I come in here for? Oh, yeah. Would you say you spend eighty percent of your work time in the studio and twenty percent in the house? Less? More?"

Lexie thought for a moment. She'd never considered this before. "Make it seventy percent studio."

"Okay." He started to leave then paused at the

door. "I'll need copies of your utility bills for the past five years. Would they also be in the envelopes?"

"Er, probably."

He nodded and left. Through the window, Lexie watched him walk back across the lawn to the kitchen door and disappear inside the house. He had a great ass. And great shoulders. Long legs. Narrow hips. Really, he was perfectly proportioned. She wouldn't mind painting him nude….

Stop it. She was behaving like a…a cougar. She hated that term. It was so predatory.

She turned back to the canvas. Contrasting note, huh? He might actually have something there. The trick was hitting the *right* note.

Lexie mulled it over while she continued to search the studio for the envelopes. At the end of half an hour she had no further clues to her painting. Hadn't located the envelopes, either. Giving up, she grabbed a pad of heavy paper and a handful of pencils and went back inside the house. Sometimes when she sketched at random, ideas came to her.

Rafe was carrying a large purple cardboard box over to the coffee table when she walked into the living room. "I found this in your hall closet."

Lexie recognized the all-purpose box she'd bought at a stationery store. She tossed stuff in there to get it out of sight. Sinking onto the couch, she propped herself on a layer of cushions and tucked her legs beneath her skirt. She doubted he'd find any receipts in there but looking would keep him busy.

She opened the sketch pad, intending to play around with ideas, drawing things she associated with Sienna—a stethoscope, Venus on the half shell. Instead she found herself studying Rafe as he opened the box. As if anticipating treasure, his eyes gleamed.

With a 4B pencil she drew dramatic slashes of black, blocking in his thick eyebrows. Working quickly, she captured his face in a few bold strokes. Not satisfied with the jaw, she smudged out the line with her gum eraser and made it sharper, the angle steeper. Then she chose a finer pencil to work in the shading on the hollows of the cheeks, around the eyes, the black stubble.

As he leafed through the bits and pieces in the box he began to frown. No receipts. She hadn't thought so. He rolled his shoulders, working out the kinks.

Lexie paused. He carried a lot of tension. She could see it in the lines of his face and the set of his neck. She was the one who should be tense; she was being audited. But she was good at putting unpleasant things out of her mind. Maybe a little too good.

He dug through the box, shaking his head as he lifted out nail clippers, a pencil sharpener, a broken pedometer, a small wooden bowl, assorted colored pencils, marbles, paper clips and matchbooks.

He had eyes that slanted down at the outer corner,

an aquiline nose and a mouth that was far too sensuous for someone who worked with columns and
rows.

Glancing up, Rafe noticed her sketch pad on her
upraised knee. "What are you drawing?"

"Nothing. Just playing around." Lexie started on
his ear. Every person's whorls were different, like
fingerprints.

"Playing?" he repeated as he piled everything
back into the box. "Perhaps you don't understand
the seriousness of your situation."

Lexie stretched her legs along the length of the
couch, wriggling her bare toes.

Rafe's gaze, drawn to the movement, lingered on
her bare calves. Their gazes met for a fraction of a
second. Lexie's mind flashed back to the outline of
his thigh muscle under his pants. She drew her skirt
down. Rafe glanced away.

He cleared his throat. "You need to—" He broke
off, frowning. Apparently he was having trouble
formulating the sentence. "You need to find those
receipts if you want to offset expenses against the
income from the paintings you sold to the American.
If not, you'll be charged the maximum amount of
tax."

Lexie stilled. "What would that be?"

He started piling things back into the box. "Tax on
the forty thousand dollars, with minimal deductions,
would be around fifteen thousand."

Fifteen thousand dollars.

"Where am I going to get that kind of money?" she demanded. She may have sounded angry, but she wasn't. She was scared.

He shrugged. Not his problem, in other words.

She had to find those envelopes.

But she also had to finish Sienna's portrait. It was the best thing she'd ever done and she really thought she had a shot at winning the Archibald Prize and the fifty-thousand dollars that went to first place. Fear speared through her. She *had* to win the cash prize. She would need it to pay her tax bill.

Lexie closed her eyes and slowly breathed out all the way. Calm. Peace. Light.

"Utility bills?" Rafe reminded her.

Ooh.

"I'll go look for them now." She set her sketch pad aside and rose. He was going to be in her house for days, possibly the rest of the week. Even without being blocked it was hard to see how she was going to get any work done.

Lexie went down the hall, past her bedroom to the spare room where she kept a small whitewashed desk and a single bed covered in a patchwork quilt. Her early paintings, seascapes mainly, covered the walls. Rifling the desk drawers, she came up with…nothing. This was ridiculous even for her. She knew she didn't have five years' worth of household bills, but she'd kept some. They must be with her tax envelopes. Where were they?

She opened the double doors of the closet. Piles of old clothing she would never wear again, jigsaw puzzles—mostly with one or two pieces missing—and the hair dryer that sparked. What was wrong with her that she couldn't throw away broken and useless items? It was no wonder she could never find anything. Pretty soon she'd have to rent another house just to store the things she didn't use.

What was this? She pulled out a small antique clock. She'd forgotten she had this. It had a hand-painted white enamel face and was mounted on a rosewood base. She'd been attracted to it originally because the mechanism was exposed. Every cog, wheel and spring was visible and could be seen moving. When it worked.

"That's a skeleton clock."

She leaped back and almost dropped the thing. How long had he been standing in the doorway? "You have to stop sneaking up on me."

Rafe ignored her reaction and moved closer to get a better look. "Quite a nice example, too. My father repairs clocks for a living. He's taught me a bit over the years. Where did you get that one?"

"I must have picked it up at a flea market years ago." She looked underneath and found a tiny key taped to the base. She inserted it into the slot and wound it. Nothing happened. "It's broken," she said, disappointed.

"Let me see."

While he inspected the mechanism of springs and cogged wheels, she studied the thick black hair that fell over his forehead, the way his mouth compressed in concentration.

Suddenly, he stilled, as if aware of how close they were standing. "Speaking of time, it's getting late." He handed the clock back to her, cautious about making contact, either by skin or by eye.

Rafe walked back to the dining room. Lexie followed carrying the clock. He began packing up his briefcase. His movements appeared casual, but she noticed he was cramming papers in any old how.

"I'll be back tomorrow," Rafe said. "I suggest you keep looking—"

Someone knocked.

Before Lexie could answer it, the front door opened. Her mother, Hetty, stood on the step in a long tunic top and flowing cotton pants, a suitcase in either hand. Her spiky gray hair stood up from her head.

"Mom," Lexie said, going forward to embrace her. "What are you doing here? Is everything all right?"

"No, it's not," Hetty said tartly. "Your father and I had a terrible fight. I'm moving in with you." She stepped inside, and noticed Rafe. "Sorry. I didn't know you had company."

"He's not company, he's—" Lexie broke off. *"Moving in?"*

RAFE SLIPPED OUT while Lexie bombarded her mother with questions and Hetty made vague and weary responses. He got behind the wheel of his ten-year-old Mazda and had to slam the door twice before it would stay shut.

He glanced at his fishing rod lying across the backseat. That would have to wait another day. He was tired and Murphy, his dog, would be waiting for him. As it was, he had to drive home in the late-afternoon heat through the tail end of rush hour traffic. With the windows rolled down because the air-conditioning didn't work, he headed north, away from Melbourne's bayside suburbs and into the Dandenong Mountains.

Mulling over the day, he found himself worrying about Lexie, if she would find her envelopes, if she could pay her taxes—

He was doing it again. Getting involved, feeling compassion.

Hell.

"YOUR TAX AUDITOR is rather gorgeous." Hetty dumped her suitcase on the antique quilt covering the single bed in Lexie's spare room. "Where did you find him?"

"He's not mine, he belongs to the government. And he's turning my house upside down," Lexie said from the doorway. "I wish he was never coming back."

Did she? Or was she already thinking she'd wash her hair tonight.

"It's no fun being audited but surely it's just a matter of letting him do his job." Hetty opened her suitcase and started to unpack.

"The problem is, I can't find the envelopes that have all my tax receipts in them. They're somewhere in the house but I have no idea where. Plus I'm going to have to pay back taxes with money I don't have. Plus I have to finish Sienna's portrait because the deadline for the Archibald is coming up and I can't tell what's missing but something is. Something crucial." Lexie's voice seemed to have risen an octave. She sucked in a breath. "I've been blocked for ages. All I can do is paint stupid beach huts and make pencil sketches—"

She broke off, thinking about the sketch of Rafe and how there was a hint of something tragic in his eyes. She would try to capture that tomorrow. No, she wouldn't. Tomorrow she would work on Sienna. Or find the envelopes.

"Oh, God. My life is unfolding like a Greek tragedy."

"Don't overdramatize. Everything will be fine."

Hetty draped a cotton blouse over a hanger. "I know you. You get blocked and it feels as if it'll be forever. Then one day something clicks and away you go again."

Lexie slumped onto the bed. "I hope you're right."

Hetty went to hang the blouse and clicked her tongue at the crowded closet. She pushed through the hangers and brought out a faded pink dress. "Honestly, Lexie, I recognize this from when you went to art school. Why not get rid of it?"

Lexie's mouth dried as she recalled being seventeen and living away from home in her first year at art school. She'd bought the dress because the cut was loose and hid her thickening waist. No one in her family knew, then or now, that she'd been pregnant.

"It holds memories. I—I can't throw it away." The crush of soft fabric between her fingers brought a sudden rush of grief and guilt. Why did she torture herself by keeping it around? She should get rid of it. In fact…

What if it was all the excess stuff in her house that was blocking her? Declutter. Wasn't that what all the women's magazines were telling her to do?

"On second thought…" Lexie grabbed the pink dress and an armful of hangers and hauled them out of the closet.

Seeing space open up felt good. With a burst of

enthusiasm she took down the folded piles of clothes from the shelf and threw them into the hallway along with the clothes on hangers. This might be another form of procrastination but at least it would achieve something.

"What's going on with you and Dad?" she asked, standing on tiptoe to reach the jigsaw puzzles. "I thought you wanted to get back together with him. I thought you were going to give him another chance."

"He's not giving *me* another chance," Hetty said, hanging up her blouses in the space Lexie'd created. "Even though Smedley is fine, Steve still blames me for the dog eating fox bait." Hetty's voice wobbled. "Steve wouldn't even look at me at the Fun Run. It's been two weeks now and we barely speak. While I was at the yoga retreat in Queensland he converted our house to a bachelor pad complete with car parts on the kitchen floor and a pool table in the living room."

"Get him to change it back."

"He's never home to do anything! He's out all the time, volunteering at the Men's Shed Jack founded, at Toastmasters meetings…."

"You wanted him to find a hobby," Lexie reminded her.

"He's found a hobby all right." Lexie read the anger in Hetty's gray eyes. "Her name is Susan Dwyer."

Huh? Lexie dropped the puzzle boxes on top of the

pile of clothes. Steve, her stolid conservative father, the man who'd been dependent on Hetty for years, had another woman? "No way. Dad wouldn't have an affair."

Hetty lifted her shoulders, her mouth twisting. "What do you call it when he's out with her three nights of the week? He *says* they're on a committee to organize some speech contest or other. And he *says* she's his mentor and is helping him with his entry. But he's not the type to get caught up in committees. He has to be doing it because of her."

"Not necessarily," Lexie said, trying to be fair. "Renita and I went to the Toastmasters meeting the night he did his Icebreaker speech. It was obvious he enjoys the meetings and *everyone* there, not just Susan Dwyer." She paused before adding, "He really has changed while you've been in Queensland. Maybe you don't know him as well as you think you do."

"I don't know him at all anymore." Hetty burst into tears. "Lexie, what am I going to do?"

"It'll be all right." Dismayed, Lexie pulled her mother into a hug. "You wanted him to be more self-sufficient."

"I didn't want him to stop needing me." Hetty hiccupped on a sob. "Or loving me."

"He loves you. He needs you," Lexie said helplessly. Her father had been through a lot in the past six months, including being diagnosed with type two diabetes. Renita had encouraged him to join the gym and start jogging. Steve had taken up Toastmasters of his own accord as a way to get out and meet people. He was a completely different person from the overweight depressed man who couldn't adjust to retirement. Everything should have been great for him and Hetty.

"You changed when you took up yoga," Lexie reminded her mother, easing back to meet Hetty's gaze. "You need to let him change, too."

"You're right." Hetty blinked, sniffed, dragged in a shuddering breath. "I need to learn to accept him as he's becoming. Even if it means that from now on we follow different paths."

"Wait a minute. *No*," Lexie said, alarmed. "You'll get back together. You have to. You can't throw away forty years of marriage."

"I don't want to," Hetty said. "But right now, I can't live at home."

Lexie gave her mum another hug. "Stay here as long as you want. You could help me look for my receipts."

She didn't want to mention she was low on groceries or that she had a cash flow problem. With luck she would sell a painting this week. The seascapes she did were bread and butter between the odd commission she got for portraits.

"I'll pay rent, of course," Hetty said, somehow reading her mind.

"Don't even think about it," Lexie said. "But I'd

love you to show me some of the new yoga techniques you learned at the retreat."

"Gladly." Hetty gave her a watery smile.

Lexie released her mother. She picked up the bundle of clothes in the hallway and carried them to the front door. First thing tomorrow she would donate them to the thrift shop.

She was already beginning to feel lighter. It was good to start afresh. With a clearer mind she might find the key to finishing Sienna's portrait.

But as she walked toward the spare room her footsteps slowed.

Lexie reached the box of clothes and removed the pink dress. She took it to her bedroom and hung it at the back of her closet.

CHAPTER THREE

"WHAT THE HELL'S going on, Murph?" Rafe said as he pulled up in front of Lexie's house the next morning. Bulging plastic garbage bags were piled along the path. Boxes of odds and ends were stacked behind her car. The front door was propped open. Was she turning the house inside out in her search for the envelopes?

He parked at the curb and unloaded his briefcase and a couple bags of groceries. Murphy, his black-and-white mutt, scampered at his heel, sniffing boxes, relieving himself on the gardenia bush, barking at the brown cat that hissed at him before darting into the shrubbery.

Rafe stopped. The skeleton clock was in one of the boxes clearly destined for rubbish. He tucked it under his arm and knocked on the open door. Soft music was playing and vanilla incense drifted through the house. "Lexie?"

"Come in." Her voice sounded constricted.

Rafe slipped off his shoes and walked through the hall, turning left into the living room. The coffee table and armchair had been pushed back so Lexie and her mother had space for yoga. Hetty was in a deep lunge, arms outstretched. Lexie was standing on one leg, doubled over and touching the floor. Her other long and shapely leg straight up in the air, toe pointed. Her hair hung in a curtain around her head.

It was rude to stare but he couldn't help it. Lexie's aqua blue tank top and low-slung cropped pants fit her like a second skin, molding to every slender curve. Man, she could bend.

Cool it, Ellersley. Independent state of mind, remember?

Positioning his briefcase in front of him, he began to recite the Taxation Administration Act of 1953 in his head. Murphy settled onto his haunches at Rafe's feet.

Lexie lowered her leg with exquisite control and straightened, flipping her hair back. "Rafe, I found the envelopes!"

"Excellent." His name on her lips, her excitement… *Pursuant to Schedule A, Section D, the party of the first part shall pay a portion of their income to the Commonwealth of Australia, calculated for the financial period from the first day of July to the thirtieth day of June…*

Then, before he could ask where the envelopes were, Lexie noticed Murphy. "Oh, my God, a stray followed you in. Quick, get him out before he goes after Yin and Yang." She came at him, making shoo-ing motions. "Go on, bad doggy, out!"

Murphy started licking her hands. She snatched her hands away.

"This is Murphy," Rafe said. "Sorry, I should have asked first if I could bring him here. I couldn't leave him home alone for days on end. He's a good boy. He likes cats."

Likes to annoy them. The truth was, Rafe had forgotten all about Lexie's Burmese cats.

"All right," Lexie said reluctantly. "But if they get stressed, he'll have to stay in the backyard." She noticed the grocery bags. "What's this?"

"I thought I'd pick up a few things since I'll be around a lot this week. You know how crabby I get when I'm hungry." His conscience wouldn't allow him to go out to eat knowing she was lunching on two-minute noodles.

Hetty straightened out of her yoga pose. "Hello," she said, extending her hand. "I'm Hetty. I arrived yesterday just as you were leaving."

"Pleased to meet you officially," he said, shaking hands.

Lexie peeked inside the grocery bags at the meat, cheese, eggs, fruit and vegetables he'd bought. She gazed at him, her eyes so dazzling they were hard to look at and impossible to turn away from. "You didn't have to do this."

"So," he said, rubbing his hands together like some

cartoon character because otherwise he'd reach out and touch her or do something equally inappropriate. "Show me to the envelopes."

"Ta-da!" She gestured grandly to the dining table.

Rafe's heart plummeted to the soles of his croc skins.

Holy shit.

Manila envelopes full to bursting were stacked four high and five or six wide. There must be dozens of them. As he looked, a precariously balanced envelope slid off the top of the pile and fell on the floor.

"I'll put away the groceries." Hetty picked up the bags and carried them to the kitchen.

"Thanks, Mum," Lexie said.

Rafe walked over to the table and picked up one of the bulging envelopes. "Where did you find them?"

"In the garden shed," she said excitedly. "I remembered where they were in the middle of the night. You know how sometimes you wake up and the answer to something that's been puzzling you is right there, clear as a bell? I woke up with a picture in my mind of me shoving them on the potting table."

The woman was certifiable.

And she was standing too close. Her perfume combined with the scent of her warm skin was stirring his hormones. Occasionally he was attracted to women he audited, but until Lexie they'd always been easy

to resist. All he could think of right now was wanting
to grab her and kiss her breathless.

He'd never encountered anyone like her—sexy
and exasperating in almost equal measures. "Why
would you put them in the garden shed?"

"They were driving me nuts. I had to paint." Her
gaze seemed to get stuck on the open neck of his
shirt. "Out of sight, out of mind."

"What if you needed to garden?" And didn't that
just make him picture her kneeling in the garden bed,
her ass in the air?

"It was the middle of the summer." She gathered
her hair in a bunch and let it fall down her back.
He followed the line of her upraised arms with his
eyes. "The, um, grass doesn't even need mowing.
Because…it doesn't get enough water. To grow."

"That's…logical."

With difficulty, Rafe dragged his eyes back to
the envelope. Opening it, he pulled out a handful of
loose pieces of paper. "You must spend a lot on art
supplies."

"They're not all from buying art supplies. I'm
never sure what's allowable and what isn't, so just to
be on the safe side, I keep every receipt I get."

"O-kay. Every receipt?" he echoed faintly, feeling
a sharp twinge in his stomach. He put the envelope
down and opened his briefcase. He found that if he
avoided looking at her, it was easier to concentrate.

"I'll go through them with you," Lexie said. "But

first, I've got to take a load of stuff to the thrift store. I've got to declutter. I can't think."

"I'll help," Hetty volunteered, returning from the kitchen.

"Thanks, Mum." Lexie abandoned the receipts, grabbed her purse from the table and headed for the front door. She yelled over her shoulder, "I'll be back."

Hetty took a seat at the table and gazed expectantly at Rafe. "What would you like me to do?"

Rafe scanned the slips of paper in his hand and shook his head. Lexie had put receipts from different years in the same envelope. "You could start sorting these by year."

Murphy was doing the rounds of the living room, sniffing at every chair. Yin watched him through slitted green eyes from the arm of the couch. "Murphy, here." The dog trotted over and lay at his feet under the table.

Hetty started separating the receipts into piles. "I don't mind telling you the family has been worried about Lexie's finances. Ever since she quit teaching to paint full-time she's had trouble making ends meet. But she refuses to accept help. She says she made the decision to be an artist, and she's willing to live with the consequences. It's nice of you to come to her house and do this for her."

"It's my job." He wondered if he should mention

that Lexie would likely cop a fine. He felt bad about that—

Not his problem. Feeling sorry for the taxpayer was how he'd gotten into trouble over his last audit.

He heard Lexie return for another box. A moment later he heard her car start.

Rafe called up the spreadsheet onto the screen. He pulled a calculator out of his briefcase and began entering numbers. When he'd done all he could, he reached for an envelope and began sorting. There were receipts for the hairdresser (not deductible), art gallery entry (deductible), a car battery (debatable)—

"Do you live locally?" Hetty asked.

"Sassafras, up in the Dandenongs. But I'm booked into a bed and breakfast just down the road."

"Myrna Bailey's, right?" She waited for him to nod then went on, "Do you have family?"

Rafe suppressed a sigh. What was it about middle-aged women that they had to know everything about a person? That they couldn't sit at the same table without making conversation. "My parents live in Western Victoria, in Horsham. I have a sister in Brisbane."

"Do your parents farm?"

It was a natural enough question given the location but he hated answering it. His parents, Darryl and Ellen, had moved to the country years ago, after Darryl's accident, because it was cheaper than the city. Rafe always wanted to explain that although his father was in a wheelchair, there'd been a time when he'd had bigger dreams.

"No, my father has a home-based business repairing clocks and watches." He should go see them. It had been months since he'd last been out there.

Rafe continued sifting through Lexie's receipts. He came across an application form for an artist's society. He noted down the amount of annual dues and saw she'd filled in her birth date.

Before he could censor himself, he blurted, "Is Lexie really thirty-eight years old?"

"Yes," Hetty said. "It was her birthday last month."

Twelve years older than him. He'd figured she was older but not by *that* much.

"She looks a lot younger."

"It's the yoga and the meditation," Hetty said. "Plus she has a naturally serene disposition. Nothing bothers her."

"The portrait she's painting is bothering her."

"Well, yes," Hetty conceded.

Rafe sat back in his chair, still staring at the year Lexie was born. She could have easily passed for thirty. If that was the result of meditation and yoga maybe he ought to take it up. Or not.

Twelve years.

He added the art society annual dues to the column. Afternoon sun shone through the crystals hanging from the window frame, making rainbows on his page of numbers. There seemed to be crystals everywhere in the house. He'd noticed them in the kitchen, too. From below the table, Murphy snored.

"Do you have a wife or girlfriend?" Hetty asked.

Rafe stifled another sigh. "Never married. No girlfriend at present."

"You're young yet," she said comfortably. "There's plenty of time to marry and have children."

The other thing about middle-aged women was, they wanted to marry a guy off and tie him down with kids before he'd had a chance to enjoy life. What was up with that?

He stabbed at the keypad on his calculator. "How are you doing with the sorting?"

"Don't you like kids?"

"I beg your pardon?"

"I *said,* you have plenty of time to marry and have kids," Hetty recapped patiently, as she dealt out receipts like playing cards at a bridge game. "*You* didn't reply. So then I asked, don't you like children?"

How did she get child-hater from silence? There'd been nothing to say in response to her statement so he hadn't bothered with meaningless chatter. "Kids are fine, I guess. As long as they're other people's."

Tamsin, his ex-girlfriend, had made him gun-shy. They'd been together nearly a year when she'd gotten clucky. Then he'd discovered she'd "accidentally" forgotten to take her birth control pills and the huge fight that ensued had killed their relationship. Fortunately, she hadn't got pregnant.

Feeling Hetty's gaze on him, he could sense the questions forming in her mind. "I've got plans, okay? I'm not ready to get married *or* have children. Maybe in ten years I'll think about it. But first I want to start my own fishing charter business."

"That's interesting," she said, leaning forward, chin on her palm. "When are you going to do that?"

"Next year, if all goes well." Then he pointedly began entering numbers into his calculator. He'd had enough soul baring for one day. And he'd jeopardize his job if he didn't do this audit properly.

Hetty went back to sorting receipts. The only sound was the clicking of the keys as Rafe entered data.

After a few minutes her hands stilled. Out of the blue she said, "I've lost touch with my husband." She stared at the receipts in her hand.

Fresh pain stabbed his stomach. Now she expected *him* to ask *her* questions. News flash! He wasn't a woman. Hell. Why did she have to look so unhappy? "What happened?" he asked heavily.

"We grew apart when we weren't looking," she said, launching into what was sure to be a long-winded explanation. "We'd been up and down for six months or more, ever since we retired. Then I went away to Queensland for a yoga retreat. He didn't like that. Now that I'm back, well, he doesn't seem to need me anymore."

She paused, apparently waiting for another response.

"Has he said he doesn't need you?" Rafe asked gruffly. "Sometimes women read stuff into things that guys don't mean."

"No, but—"

"Did he tell you to leave?"

"I told you, I left him. I share the blame, I do." She waved a veined hand weighted with silver rings. "But I'm ready to try again. Only he has a whole new life and there doesn't seem to be any place in it for me." Her large gray eyes swam with tears. "He doesn't care if I'm here or not. He won't talk to me, barely looks at me. Forty years of marriage and it's over. I'm pretty sure there's another woman. I don't know what to do."

Rafe just nodded. Why was she confiding in him? He was no marriage counselor.

"If I was your husband," he improvised, hoping that a solution would shut her up. "I'd want you to prove you would never go away again before I took you back."

Hetty blinked away moisture. "How can I do that?"

"By going home and staying put. By not running off to your daughter's house. It takes time to win back trust."

Hetty stared. "For a young man you're very wise."

She started sorting again. After ten minutes she put down the receipts. "He's got to meet me halfway. Talk to me, for a start. Listen to how I feel."

Rafe grunted. His calculator clicked steadily.

Hetty's voice flowed on.

THE HOUSE WAS QUIET when Lexie entered an hour later. Odd. Her mother liked to chat. She'd thought Hetty would be talking Rafe's ear off. Peering into the living room, she could see that Rafe was alone, his back to her, bent over the table. His computer sat idle.

She dropped her purse on the hall table and kicked off her shoes. "I'm back. Where's Mum?"

He straightened and glanced over his shoulder, brushing a thick strand of black hair out of his eyes. "No idea. She said something but I wasn't listening. I think she left."

He was working on the skeleton clock. His shirt-sleeves were rolled up over forearms smattered with dark hair. His hands were well shaped, his long fingers delicately manipulating the inner workings with a tiny screwdriver and tweezers.

She sank into the chair next to him.

"I replaced a spring, tightened a few things." He sat back. From the compartment at the bottom of the base he took the small key and inserted it into the keyhole. He turned it a few times and listened.

The clock started to tick.

Rafe grunted with satisfaction and glanced sideways at her.

Lexie's eyes blurred. The clock wasn't going to help her finish her portrait or do her taxes but it felt like the first thing that had gone right in days. Maybe weeks. "You did it."

As if he'd fixed her life.

Without stopping to think she leaned over, put her hands on his shoulders and kissed him.

CHAPTER FOUR

KISSING HIM was like touching her lips to a live electrical wire. A current flowed through her, lifting her off her chair and onto her feet. Rafe surged upward, too, his hands framing her face as he pressed his mouth to hers in a long breathless kiss. She slid her arms around his neck. He gathered her close, pressing hot kisses to her cheeks, her nose, her neck. Then his mouth found hers again and his tongue plunged inside, flooding her with heat and sensation…

Her hands slid down his shirtfront, pushing against his chest. "Stop," she gasped.

Instantly, he released her, breathing hard, eyes wild. "I shouldn't have done that."

Aghast, Lexie fled down the hall to her bedroom. She slammed the door shut and paced between the end of the bed and the closet. Rafe was a government tax accountant here to audit her, not to…to…

She breathed in deeply and slowly, taking the air all the way to her stomach. Then she let it out through her mouth. Normally that would calm her. Not quite.

Another breath. She would go back out there, act

normally and not do anything dumb. Shoulders back and down, she opened the door.

Rafe was standing on the other side, fist raised to knock. Face-to-face. She stared. *That mouth.*

"I'm *so* sorry," she said, the words tumbling out. "I don't know what came over me. That was inappropriate. Please forget it ever happened. I'll go out to my studio. Stay out of your way. I go a little crazy when I'm not working. Please don't think anything of it."

She paused for breath.

"What just happened out there?" He looked shell-shocked, as if he hadn't taken in a word she'd said.

"That's what I'm trying to explain," she babbled. "I didn't mean to kiss you. Well, obviously on one level I did. I've been thinking of it all day. And yesterday—"

"I've been thinking about nothing else." His dazed eyes settled on her mouth. "I only know two things. I shouldn't be doing this. And I don't want to stop." He kissed her again. "Tell me to stop." His voice was low and rasping. Almost pleading.

Holding his gaze, she took his hands and settled them on her hips. The heat of his fingers burned through her thin cotton yoga pants. He drew her closer.

Rafe glided the tip of his tongue into the hollow behind her ear. His mouth moved over her neck, his breath warm against her skin.

"I don't want you to stop." Easing back, she met his hot dark eyes and melted. "I want to go to bed with you."

He went still. Lexie felt every hair on her body stand on end. She held her breath.

"I should not be doing this," he said again, stripping his shirt off. Underneath he wore a white T-shirt that accentuated his tanned shoulders and strapping chest.

If he was prey to her cougar, he was willing prey.

Her nerves jumping, she stepped back, pulling him toward her by his belt. Kissing him as he stumbled forward. Her breath got stuck somewhere between her throat and her chest as she worked his buckle.

And then he was shucking off his gray trousers and tossing them, along with his shirt. Lexie drank in the sight of him. Her last lover had been in his forties with the beginnings of a paunch and a softening jawline. Although a hard body wasn't everything, Rafe's smooth skin, sculpted muscles and erection were just…wow.

She practically tore her clothes off, trembling with need, almost unable to stand. She pushed down his black boxers as he fumbled her bra off. He cupped her breasts in his hands, sucking hard on one nipple, as he slid her panties over her hips. They were both naked, pressing against each other, so hot she could swear she heard her skin sizzle against his.

"Oh, hell," he groaned into her ear. His hands tightened. "I don't have any condoms. Do you?"

"No. But I have an IUD." She rested her forehead against his chest, breathing hard, praying they weren't stopping now. "I'm healthy." She glanced up, searching his eyes. "You?"

He met her gaze straight on. "Yeah, I'm good."

Growling low in her throat, she pulled him down on top of her on the bed in a tangle of limbs, tongues and hands. She was aching to feel him inside her. His biceps tensed as he poised over her. His thighs nudged between hers. So much power, so much heat. Lexie ran her restless hands over his hips, urging him.

Thick and hard, he plunged. Lexie thrust her hips upward until he filled her completely. She savored the delicious sensation, her legs trembling with strain.

He thrust again, grinding into her, his breath hot against her cheek. "Tell me if I'm too rough."

She was so aroused she couldn't speak.

His low voice rumbled next to her ear, saying wicked things that made her laugh and gasp. And all the time he was moving, pumping, hard and fast.

She climaxed quickly in a white heat that obliterated everything but the waves of pleasure pulsing through her. Dimly she was aware of Rafe, every muscle taut as he strained above her. And then an unearthly groan as he spilled himself into her.

RAFE OPENED his eyes. In the dim light of Lexie's bedroom he could see her tangled blond hair, a bare shoulder and a small square of pillow. He nuzzled her neck, breathed in her scent.

He rolled over onto his back. She stirred sleepily and rolled with him, draping an arm across his chest.

Suddenly he felt very cold.

What the hell had he been thinking?

Obviously, he hadn't been thinking.

He didn't *want* to think. He wanted to bury himself in Lexie again. To trace the whorls of the shell tattoo on her hip with his tongue, to dip lower, licking his way up the slender muscle of her inner thigh. He was getting hard again just thinking about it.

Larry didn't have to hear about this.

Not if Rafe did the audit properly, everything aboveboard. No fudging to save Lexie money. No going easy on her, overlooking the odd painting sale to reduce her income. After all, she wasn't expecting anything like that—

Was she?

He felt even colder. Could she have seduced him so he'd reduce her taxes? People tried offering much less with the same expectation.

Nah. That was crazy. She wasn't the type.

On the other hand, how well did he really know her?

LEXIE PEERED over the mound of files between her and Rafe. The best sex she'd ever had, bar none. This morning, though, he was ignoring her. He'd barely looked at her.

"Can I claim video rentals?" she asked.

Rafe kept his head down, the calculator clicking nonstop. "Did they inspire you to paint?"

"Everything inspires me." She frowned at the receipt in her hand. "Except doing my taxes."

"Claim the video."

She dropped it on the Save pile.

Theirs was just a fling, she knew that. Rafe was a government tax agent. She'd known him for all of two days. As soon as the audit was over he'd be hitting the road.

Anyway, he was too young for her.

"Dinner at the pub?" she asked, moving on to the next receipt.

"Not unless it was a meeting with a gallery owner or a potential buyer or somehow business-related."

She tossed the receipt in the rubbish bin. Going through receipts was the most boring thing in the world. Her gaze kept drifting to Rafe. She wanted to go over there and wrestle him to the ground and kiss him until he cried uncle.

She rose restlessly, and paced through the living room, coming to a halt at the bookshelf. The quietly ticking skeleton clock caught her eye. She carried it back to the table.

Lexie laid her chin on her folded hands and studied the series of linked wheels of decreasing size. In the time it took the largest wheel to turn a quarter of the way around, the next wheel had spun a full circle and the next one down had gone around five times. The final wheel turned a spring that was coiled in a loose spiral that expanded and contracted with each click of a cog.

Like a heartbeat.

The minute hand ticked over to twelve and the hour hand pointed to three. There was a whirring noise and a tiny hammer struck a chime.

She glanced up to share her delight and found Rafe watching her. *Finally,* he was looking at her. "Do you want to…" She nodded in the direction of her bedroom.

A red flush spread across his cheeks. "I have to get this finished."

God, what was wrong with her? She shouldn't have been so direct. She was scaring him. But they couldn't just act as if nothing had happened. Last night they'd stopped long enough to eat dinner then had gone back to bed. He'd gotten up before she awoke and went back to his B&B.

"I know what's going on," she said. "You're feeling guilty because you're not supposed to sleep with clients."

"Something like that." he muttered.

"That doesn't mean you have to ignore me," she said matter-of-factly. "Last night was amazing. Can't we just accept that we have this freakish natural chemistry and enjoy it until you have to ride into the sunset?"

He put down his calculator and dragged a hand across his face. With his chin in his palm, he stared at her. "I can't reduce your taxes because we slept together."

It took a moment for that to sink in. "Is that what you think?" she demanded, surging to her feet. Slips of paper fluttered to the floor. "You think I'm hoping you'll give me some sort of concession for…for services rendered?"

Rafe started to shake his head. "I—"

"I'm an artist, not a… Oh!" she exclaimed, hands clenched. "I can't believe you'd even suggest such a thing."

She brushed past him, striding through the kitchen and across the backyard. Sorting receipts was bullshit. She needed to at least attempt to paint.

Inside her studio she paced some more, trying to calm down. Of all the arrogant assholes. He had a hell of a nerve saying that to her after the things they had done together. He should have said no last night if he was so worried about his precious integrity.

Sienna's portrait struck her as terrible, no good at all. Maybe if she started over, layering in the background before she even began on the face….

Her large canvases, stretched onto wooden frames, were on top of the high cupboard. Jack had put them there for her, out of the way. Dragging a stool over, she climbed onto it and reached up. Her fingertips brushed the edge of the top canvas. Frustrated, she stretched onto tiptoe, leaning closer.

"Lexie," Rafe said from behind her.

Startled, she glanced over her shoulder. The shift in her balance made the stool rock dangerously. Arms flailing, she tried to catch herself. Rafe ran forward but she was able to right herself before he could help.

"I was fine until you yelled," she snapped. "Don't sneak up on me like that. In fact, better not come near me at all. I might try to seduce you again."

"I'm sorry." He stood below her, awkwardly. "I didn't mean to insult you."

"Well, you did!" She slowly got down. God help her, she still wanted him. Realizing that only made her angrier.

"The fact remains, I shouldn't have slept with you," he said. "It isn't just some company policy, this is the government. Tax agents are supposed to maintain an independent state of mind. We can't allow ourselves to be bribed with expensive scotch or restaurant meals—"

"I wasn't trying to bribe you." She glared at him.

"I admitted I was wrong. I apologized." He spun away and back again. "I don't know what more you want from me."

"I want you to kiss me."

He stared at her. "Kiss you? Are you trying to make me lose my mind?" Then with a groan he took her in his arms.

Lexie pressed her lips to his. But she'd barely registered the earthy scent of his skin, the firmness of his lips, the heat rising between them, when he abruptly pulled away, leaving her gasping.

"I can't concentrate when I'm around you. And if we're in bed, I'm not getting your audit done." He sank onto the same stool she'd just got off and propped his elbows on his knees. "What am I going to do?"

"Kiss me," she repeated.

"I don't think you fully understand just what's coming once I finish the audit. You're going to owe a lot of money. In my experience people tend to want to shoot the messenger."

"I'm not going to blame you for my mistake," she said, pushing a hand through his hair. "*I* did the wrong thing, not filing a tax return."

"Not just wrong. It's illegal," he reminded her. "There will be a fine."

"I don't usually jump into bed with every hot guy that comes along." She took his hand and flipped it over, placing hers on top, palm to palm. She could feel the energy flow from him to her, feel the surge of heat in her blood. Her eyes met his. She could tell he felt it, too.

Lexie believed in letting the things that were meant to happen, happen.

"I. Can't. Do. This," Rafe said.

She released his hand. "All right. If that's the way it has to be."

"Good." He sounded weary. Relieved and regretful at the same time. "I'll take the envelopes back to my bed and breakfast and work on them there."

Lexie turned away. "Fine. You know the way out."

RAFE LEANED back and stretched his arms over his head. He'd set up his laptop on the small table at the bed and breakfast. The cozy sitting room contained a pair of love seats, a coffee table and a kitchenette with coffee-making facilities. A door opened into a bedroom where a light glowed in the en suite.

Envelopes and piles of receipts were spread over the furniture and the floor. He'd gotten a lot done without Lexie around to distract him. Lunch had been a toasted tomato sandwich while he worked and he'd ordered take-out Thai food for dinner.

Now it was nearly eight o'clock. Murphy had lain with his muzzle on his paws staring hopefully at him for the past hour.

"All right, Murphy. Let's go for a walk."

Hearing the magic word, Murphy sprang to his feet, ears pricked. He ran and picked up his lead where it was lying by the sliding glass doors. Rafe attached it to the dog's collar and put on his running shoes.

The evening was still warm. The setting sun gave the sky a ruddy glow as he walked the few blocks toward the bay where low, windswept tea trees grew on the cliff top. A flock of rainbow lorikeets flitted past, swooping into the gum trees. Murphy trotted at Rafe's side, making brief detours to sniff bushes, car wheels and mailboxes.

Rafe emerged onto Cliff Road and the whole of the molten bay lay before him. The sun was a crimson ball melting into the horizon and gold light glinted off the towers of Melbourne far across the water.

He didn't see her at first, he was so caught up in the sunset. Then a movement in his peripheral vision made him glance to the right. Lexie stood thirty feet away toward the cul-de-sac end of the street. She was leaning against the guardrail, her full cotton skirt fluttering in the slight breeze. The warm glow of the sun illuminated her delicate features. Tendrils of blond hair clung to her cheeks.

Slowly he walked toward her, pulling on Murphy's lead.

"Hey," she said softly, staring out at the bay. "Don't take your eyes off the sun or you'll miss the moment when it sinks below the horizon."

Rafe dutifully watched as the swollen red sun sank into the bay with astonishing speed, leaving a reddish-gold glow around the horizon.

"Do you come here to watch the sunset often?" he asked, then winced. "That sounded like a bad pickup line."

"Quite often. Especially when the moon is full. Come on. The best is still to come." Lexie took his hand, tugging him and Murphy down the road.

"Where are you taking me?"

"You'll see."

It was electrifying to walk with her cool fingers wrapped in his. This touch was deliberate. And so very wrong. Which only made it all the more exciting.

They walked past big expensive homes on the right and the bay on their left to the lookout at the end of the street. Behind them was the afterglow of the sunset. In front of them, a harvest moon was rising out of the water. It cast a glittering path to the sandy beach and the colorful beach huts. Between the sunset and the moonrise the entire sky, the houses perched among the tea trees on the cliff, and the cove, pulsed with light.

On the water, a lone kayaker stroked his way home to the sailing club.

"I wonder if that's Jack," Lexie said, leaning on the railing. "It is!" She waved and after a second the kayaker lifted a dripping paddle in salute. She turned to Rafe, her face alight. "My brother."

She stood so close in the small viewing platform

that every breath he took was filled with her scent. "I thought we'd agreed not to see each other."

She went very still. "We're just watching the sunset, Rafe."

Rafe watched as Jack beached his kayak and hoisted it over his head. He made his way up the sand to the parking lot at the sailing club. By the time he strapped it to his truck and drove away, the moon had risen above the cliff, smaller now and turning silver.

And then the sunset was just a memory.

Rafe touched Lexie's hair, feeling the silky texture of the long strands sifting through his fingers. "No one can know."

Her eyes had deepened to the same color as the sky, lit by moonlight. "No one," she repeated.

Rafe cupped her face in his hands and kissed her. Her skin beneath his palms was chill, her lips warm. His heart racing, he slipped his arm around her waist. "My room is just up the road."

CHAPTER FIVE

RAFE LED the way along the flagstone path that cut around the back of the two-story brick house. Murphy trotted ahead to wait at the wrought iron gate into the small private courtyard and the separate entrance where Rafe was able to come and go without disturbing the occupants at the house.

"This place used to belong to my ninth grade English teacher, Mrs. Bailey," Lexie murmured.

Rafe opened the gate and reached in his pocket for keys. "Myrna Bailey? Tall, iron-gray hair, sergeant-major type?"

"Yes! She must be a hundred years old by now."

"One hundred and ten." Rafe opened the sliding door. "She makes the best blueberry muffins I've ever tasted."

He flicked on a light.

"Murphy, lie down." Obediently, the dog lay on the mat at the door and rested his muzzle on his paws.

Lexie started to unbutton Rafe's shirt. "Am I going too fast?"

"No, but…" He kissed her forehead. "I can make tea if you'd like to talk for a bit." He sat on the love seat and pulled her down beside him. "This isn't just sex," he said earnestly. "I really like you."

"It's sweet that you think I need reassurance," Lexie said. "I like you, too. But this *is* just sex. Let's not kid ourselves. Besides conflict of interest, you're…well…you're too young for me."

"So, you're okay with just a fling?" he asked, not wanting any recriminations when it came time for him to leave.

"Absolutely. We're going to have a few days of the best sex of our lives."

A guy couldn't say no to that.

She leaned up to kiss him, easing off the couch. "No, you stay there." Lifting her arms, she pulled her halter top over her head.

Rafe groaned. Yoga kept her firm and toned; forgetting to eat must help keep her slim. She slipped off her panties, leaving her skirt on. Then she climbed onto his lap, facing him. Pushing her hands into his hair, she gently pulled him toward her bare breasts.

He sucked one tight pink nipple into his mouth. He loved how confident she was, how she knew exactly what she wanted and just went for it. He loved how she made him feel like a stud.

Lexie let her head fall back with a small moan. His groin tightened, throbbed. He eased down his zipper to relieve the pressure against his erection. Then he turned back to her breasts.

He skimmed his hands down her body and up

under her skirt, molding her thighs and bare buttocks. He slipped his fingers between her legs into heat and wetness. His erection surged. She rose onto her knees so he could get rid of his pants and underwear. He was so hard he hurt. A glimpse of her bare thighs beneath her skirt was the most erotic thing he'd ever seen. When he thought he couldn't stand it another second, she slid onto him, tight and hot.

Sweet relief. And then she was riding him, her breasts moving before his glazed eyes. He sucked her nipple hard, gripped her hips and pushed. Heard her cry.

And cried out himself.

RAFE GAZED into Lexie's soft blue eyes and felt foolishly proud that he'd been able to give her so much pleasure. He was pretty sure he'd satisfied her.

It had taken four times. She was awesome.

He pushed a strand of hair off her cheek. "What can I get you? A drink of water? I've got cookies in my briefcase."

She laughed at that and he felt like an idiot for sounding so young.

"Thanks but I'm not hungry." Drowsily she stroked a fingertip around his bristled chin.

Her jaw and neck were chafed red from his beard. "I didn't hurt you, did I?"

Eyes closed, she smiled dreamily. "I might not be able to walk for a week."

Rafe felt himself blush and was grateful for the low light of the bedside lamp. But she seemed to be dozing off anyway. He lay back down and pulled her in close to his side and went to sleep breathing in the scent of sex, warm skin and Lexie's hair.

LEXIE WAS DREAMING about spirals. There was the skeleton clock, with its spiral spring that expanded and contracted with every tick of the cogged wheel. Then there was the spiral at the heart of a seashell. And a double spiral of…something. Then she was dreaming about the clock again. The elegant brass whorls of the casing, the wheels connected to wheels, all turning, turning, hands moving, tick, a heartbeat, a baby's heartbeat, tick, Sienna in her blue robe not Venus but the Madonna, double helix, DNA….

The clock chimed with a preternatural volume, like a giant gong struck inside her head. Lexie swam up through the layers of her dream. She opened her eyes and sat up in bed, tingling all over.

In the darkness, cogs and wheels still moved before her eyes. Spirals turned with the illusion of upward movement.

Biological clocks.

Not her. Sienna.

No, that would be too obvious as an element in her painting. There was something else in the dream. The spiral spring at the heart of the clock. The seashell. And that other spiral, the double spiral. What had that reminded her of? An illustration from the old biology text book she found somewhere and kept as a reference.

And then it clicked.

DNA, the double helix. Two strands of genetic material, joined by molecules of…something. She couldn't remember the details, if she'd ever learned them. But she could find out. It all fit. Sienna, the mother, creating life. Sienna, the doctor, saving life. Science and Nature, hand in hand.

"That's it. I've got it," she whispered, pressing a hand to her mouth to keep from laughing. It was crystal clear now that she'd thought of it. She would paint DNA molecules in the background, so faint they would be unobtrusive, a subliminal suggestion that would imprint on the viewer's brain.

Quietly she pushed back the covers and got out of bed, shivering a little at leaving the warmth of Rafe's body. Seeing his dark head on the pillow made her smile at the memory of their lovemaking.

Four times. It was true what they said about young men.

But she couldn't stay. She had work to do.

They'd fallen asleep with the lamp on so it was easy to find her top and skirt and silently pull them on. Where were her panties? She finally found them beneath the table.

Murphy heard her and got up, stiff legged, to see

what she was doing. She patted his wiry fur and he lay down.

Rafe stirred in his sleep. Lexie held her breath. Her idea was loosely held. If she had to speak the fragile images dancing in her head might dissolve.

He settled again. She found a piece of paper and scribbled a note, which she left on the table, weighed down by her house key. Quietly she tiptoed over to turn out the light. Then she opened the sliding door an inch at a time until there was enough room for her to squeeze through.

The full moon was high overhead, illuminating the houses and gardens. Lexie walked swiftly down the middle of the empty street, listening to the sounds of the night. The bats flitted across the sky, a possum scurried along the telephone wires. She loved being out so early when everyone else was dead to the world.

Ten minutes later she let herself into her house with the spare key she kept hidden under a rock in the garden. Still charged, she showered, changed and went out back, across the lawn in her flip-flops. The grass brushed her bare ankles, prickly on her skin and damp with dew. The door to her studio stuck until she lifted it and shoved with her shoulder.

Humming, she assembled her paints and brushes, got a fresh canvas down from the shelf and found a clean palette and smock. Artificial light wasn't the best so she couldn't do more than block in the picture, but she was familar with the colors she needed and her fingers were itching to make a start. Squeezing a large blob of Cadmium Yellow onto the palette, she began.

RAFE STIRRED, eyes closed, unwilling to wake from the best sleep he'd had in ages. A grin spread across his face. He'd had no idea older women could be so hot.

Thinking about Lexie was making him hard. Eyes still closed, he reached for her.

His hand encountered only empty sheets. He opened his eyes. The pillow that bore the indentation of her head and a stray blond hair were evidence he hadn't imagined the whole thing.

Rafe propped himself on one elbow. Maybe she was in the bathroom? But no, the door was open. Everything was quiet. He could even see into the small private courtyard because he'd forgotten to pull the drapes. Empty.

She was gone.

Pushing aside a flicker of disappointment, he threw back the covers, got up and let Murphy out. Then he walked to the bathroom and set the shower on scalding. Soaping himself beneath the streaming water, he hoped he could rely on her to be discreet about the sex. He had a whole lot more to lose than she did.

LEXIE WORKED until six in the morning, slept for a couple of hours then was awake again by eight. She pottered around the kitchen, putting on the kettle, popping a slice of wholemeal bread in the toaster. Surely Sienna would be up by now. She gave her a call.

"Hello?"

"Hey, Sienna." Without further preamble Lexie asked, "What are those things that the double helix of DNA is made of? The genetic building blocks or something." She spooned vanilla yogurt into a bowl.

"Lexie?" Sienna said. In the background Lexie heard cutlery clinking, water running. "DNA…let's see. You're probably thinking of nucleotides. Each consists of a sugar, a phosphate group and a nitrogen base—either a purine or a pyrimidine."

"Whoa. I don't need the biochemistry of it, just the structure. What do they look like at a molecular level?" One-handed, she rinsed strawberries under the tap.

"Let me think… Sugars form a hexagon of carbon atoms. The phosphate group would be kind of a diagonal cross and the nitrogen bases join in the middle like the rungs of a ladder. Does that make any sense?"

"Sort of." Lexie turned the tap off. "I'd better look it up on the internet. Thanks!"

"Why are you interested in this?" Sienna asked.

"It's for your portrait. I don't want to say too much. It might not work out in the end." Hearing a knock, she said, "Someone's at the door, Sienna. I'll talk to you later."

She dried her hands and hurried out, surprised to see Hetty on the doorstep. "Where were you? Didn't you come back last night?"

"No, I was trying to make up with your father. And before you ask, no, we didn't resolve anything." Hetty moved past Lexie in a swish of wide black pants and a soft gray wrap top. She tilted her head. "How come you didn't know I wasn't here last night. Where were you?"

"Um…working on Sienna's portrait," Lexie evaded.

"You're unblocked!" Hetty gave her a quick hug. "At least something's going right."

She glanced around the messy kitchen and clucked her tongue. Taking the colander out of the sink, she started stacking Lexie's dirty dishes in it, squirting liquid soap, running hot water.

"Don't do my washing up," Lexie said. "I'll get to it."

"You'll forget now that you're painting again." Hetty reached for the dishcloth. "How are you getting along with Rafe? It can't be easy having a stranger in the house all day long."

"As a matter of fact, we're getting along rather well."

Hetty glanced over her shoulder, eyebrows raised. "What do you mean?"

"He's amazing in bed." The words just popped out of her mouth before she could stop herself. She clapped her hand over her lips. "But don't say anything. No one's supposed to know."

"Who would I tell?" Hetty turned around, her hands dripping soap. "But are you sure that's wise? He's so young."

"Is he ever!" Lexie's smile grew smug as she held up a hand showing four fingers.

Hetty's eyes widened, her mouth dropped.

"Hello?" Rafe called from the front door. "May I come in?"

"Shh. Don't let on I said anything," Lexie whispered. Raising her voice, she called out, "We're in the kitchen."

Hetty spun back to the sink. With a lot of splashing and running of water she soaped a plate.

Rafe paused in the doorway. "Good morning."

His hair was slightly damp and as he glanced at her his face colored. Lexie spared a brief regret for not staying till morning just so they could have showered together.

"Hey, Rafe. Sleep well?" With her mother's back turned she sauntered over and leaned up to kiss him on his reddening cheek.

"Where did you disappear to last night?" he murmured.

"I had a brainwave. But I can't talk about it, not until it's on the canvas." Squeezing his hand, she slipped out the back door.

RAFE FOLLOWED her progress to her studio through the window over the sink. His hand tightened on his briefcase handle. She was supposed to be discreet and here she'd just kissed him in front of her mother. Sure, Hetty's back was to them but still.

"I should just go speak with her a moment," Rafe said to Hetty as he edged toward the door. "Um, about her taxes."

"You don't have to be coy around me."

Something in her voice stopped him dead. "What did she tell you?"

"That you two were getting along well." Hetty put the dishcloth down and dried her hands. "Sit down," she said, nodding to a chair at the kitchen table. "I need to talk to you. I've been doing what you suggested but it's not working."

Oh, no, not again. Rafe cast another glance out the window but Lexie had gone inside the studio. He pulled up a bentwood chair and lowered himself into it, setting his briefcase on the floor. "Be patient with your husband. It's only been twenty-four hours."

"Steve's a stubborn man. It could be months before he breaks down and admits he still loves me. I need something that works faster. Something to get him interested in me sexually again."

Rafe rubbed the back of his neck, feeling the dampness at his hairline. "I'm not a marriage counselor. I have no expertise in this area."

"But you understand people."

"Do I? I don't understand Lexie."

"No one understands Lexie, least of all Lexie." Hetty waved that away with a flap of the tea towel. "What you said the other day resonated with me. You see, I've figured out the subtext of Steve's anger toward me. While I was away in Queensland he got sick and had to go into the hospital. Then Smedley ran away and got poisoned by eating fox bait. Steve blames me for Smedley almost dying, but I think he's really blaming me for *his* getting sick. He interpreted my trip as saying I didn't care if he lived or died. But of course he can't say that so he rants and raves about Smedley."

Rafe didn't have a clue what she was talking about. "Who's Smedley?"

"Steve's Jack Russell terrier."

"Cute dogs." Rafe nodded sagely. "Make friends with Smedley, that's my advice. Go for walks with him and Steve. Show Steve you love him *and* his dog."

Hetty sat back, the tea towel twisted in her hands. "How is that going to get us making love again?"

Rafe dropped his head in one hand and covered his face. "I'm sorry, Hetty, I haven't got a clue. If you want tax advice, I'm your man. If you want tips on the best bait for snapper or ling cod, call on me. But marriage advice? Uh-uh."

"Lexie said you were amazing in bed."

Rafe choked and went into a coughing fit. He staggered to his feet and over to the sink. Hetty got there first and ran him a glass of water.

"Here, drink that," she said.

Rafe sipped some down. When he was sure he was breathing normally, he said, "She told you that?"

"Oh, dear, I shouldn't have mentioned it. But now that I have," she went on quickly, "what do you suggest I do to turn Steve on?"

Rafe took the tea towel from her and used it to mop his forehead. "Please, there must be someone else you can ask."

"I can't go to my son or my other daughter's fiancé. That would be embarrassing for them at family dinners."

"You think?" Rafe murmured faintly.

"I'm asking because you're a man—and virile according to Lexie—and a stranger. Although I do feel oddly comfortable with you. Perhaps we knew each other in a previous life."

"Okay, well…" He racked his brain trying to think of what to say, then remembered Lexie telling him, "I want to go to bed with you." That had done it for him. "Be direct with Steve. Maybe he's not sure *you* want *him*. Tell him flat out. You might be surprised at his reaction."

"Isn't that a lot of pressure to put on a man?" Hetty asked dubiously.

"Not if he's at all interested. And for a man that basically means if he has a pulse." Then doubt assailed him. What did he know about sexual relationships in long-term marriages? He wasn't even sure if his parents had sex anymore. "Maybe you could have some Viagra on hand."

"If I did that he might think I'm saying he's got erectile dysfunction." Hetty frowned. "What about sexy lingerie? Do you think that would work?"

Rafe couldn't help picturing Lexie in skimpy lace and satin. "It would for me. Not you, of course. I mean, not that you're not—" He broke off, sweating.

"I know what you mean, dear, don't worry. Let me see if I've got all this," Hetty said, counting off on her fingers. "Suck up to the dog, don't beat around the bush and channel my inner courtesan."

Rafe blew out a gusty breath. "That about sums it up."

"What do you think about pole dancing? Sex toys?"

"I think you've got enough going on." Rafe picked up his briefcase and started to back out of the room. "I'd better get to work on the audit."

"I thought you wanted to talk to Lexie?"

"Er, that can wait. I don't want to disturb her if she's painting."

"Well, *I'm* going to disturb her," Hetty announced,

rising, too. "She can spare an hour to go shopping with me." She put down her tea towel and walked out the back door to the studio.

Rafe sat at the dining room table and unpacked his briefcase. He was up to his elbows in receipts and trying without much success not to think about Lexie's mother pole dancing in a corset and garters when Lexie came breezing into the living room with her purse slung over her shoulder.

"What did you and Mum talk about?" Lexie asked. "She's champing at the bit to get down to some specialty shop in Frankston and she swears she can't go without me."

"I wouldn't know anything about that," Rafe said. "But listen here, you can't go telling her about us. You can't tell anyone."

"Sorry, it just slipped out this morning. She sort of guessed. But don't worry. Hetty won't tell anyone else, definitely not your boss." Lexie waggled her fingers. "I'll see you later."

Lexie and Hetty left. And finally, without distractions, he began to get somewhere. The pile of envelopes he'd gone through was now greater than the pile yet to be explored. Opening a new one was like unearthing the records of some ancient civilization. He could deduce a lot about Lexie's life by the way she spent her money. Paints, restaurants, books, music, admission to art galleries, vet bills, professional dues—

Rafe heard the front door creak open. Lexie must have forgotten something. But the click of high heels didn't sound like her. She'd gone out in flat sandals.

He glanced up.

The attractive woman standing before him had bouncy brown chin-length hair and was carefully made up. Her royal-blue suit fit like a glove. She seemed as surprised to see him as he was to see her. Didn't anyone knock and wait to be invited in around here?

"Er, can I help you?" he said. "Lexie's just gone out."

"I'm Renita, her sister," the woman said. "You must be the tax man. Hetty told me about you."

Hell. What exactly had Hetty said about him? He hoped Renita wasn't looking for sex advice, too. But no, Hetty wouldn't have had time to spread that news. He hoped.

"Rafe Ellersley." He rose, extending a hand. "Australian Taxation Office."

"Is my mother here?"

"She and Lexie went shopping."

"Really? Lexie hates shopping," Renita mused. "She must still be blocked."

"Apparently she's had a brainwave. She got up in the middle of the night to paint."

"Oh?" Renita eyed him.

"That's what she told me this morning," Rafe

added quickly. All he needed was another Thatcher woman discussing his sexual relations with Lexie. They'd probably invite this Sienna person, too, and serve wine and cheese.

"Well, good for her. Listen, I dropped by to borrow Lexie's punch bowl. And to remind her we're having a barbecue for Jack and Sienna tonight at Brett's new house. They're leaving for Bali next week to get married. This will be a pre-wedding party in lieu of a reception."

"I'll pass the message on."

"Six o'clock. You can come, too, if you like. I understand you're staying in Summerside for a few days."

"I wouldn't want to intrude on a family party."

"It's not just family. There will be lots of people. Please, don't let me disturb your work. I'll just go look for the punch bowl."

She went out to the kitchen. Rafe could hear cabinet doors opening and closing, dishes and pots being moved around to a background of mild curses. He knew how she felt.

"I can't find it," Renita said, returning to the living room. She walked slowly around the room, peering into corners. "She might have used it to put pinecones or shells in. It's the kind of thing she'd do, never mind that it's Waterford crystal and fifty years old."

"Her tax files turned up in the garden shed," Rafe said.

"That doesn't surprise me." Renita straightened. "I set up a spreadsheet and accounting system for her but she didn't use it. The envelopes were the next best option. I even reminded her every year when it was time to get her taxes done. It goes in one ear and out the other."

Rafe thought back to what Lexie had said about her family. She was right. They didn't seem to have much faith in her. Granted, that seemed to be warranted.

Renita glanced at her watch. "I've got to go. Ask Lexie about the punch bowl, will you?"

HETTY GINGERLY PICKED UP a large rubber dildo in Day-Glo orange. "Do women actually use these?"

Lexie put back the tester bottle of perfumed massage oil and glanced up in surprise. "Don't you have one?"

"I've always had your father until recently."

The shop's aisles were crowded with sex products but at midmorning on a weekday, Lexie and Hetty were the only customers.

Lexie reached for another tester, wondering if Rafe was a musky or a citrusy kind of guy. She shut her eyes, casting her mind back to his sex-warmed skin. His was more of an exotic spicy note. Cumin and coriander with a hint of chili. She sniffed another tester. Perfect. She would enjoy rubbing this over his body. And then rubbing herself over him.

The shop assistant, a thirty-something woman

with a glossy black bob, piercings and tattoos, approached Hetty. "Do you know what you're looking for in a dildo?"

"Not really," Hetty said. "What do you recommend?"

Lexie stood back as the sales girl talked her mother into buying the Orgasmitron 500.

CHAPTER SIX

LEXIE CAME THROUGH the front door and dropped her packages in the hall. Rafe was still seated at the dining table, bent over her files. She put her arms around him from behind and began kissing his neck.

"Renita would like to borrow the punch bowl," he told her, continuing to enter numbers. "She looked around but couldn't find it."

"It's in the linen closet." Lexie blew on his ear.

"Of course it is," he murmured. "Is Hetty with you? Your sister was looking for her, too."

"She went home to try out her new dildo."

Rafe held up a hand. "Too much information."

"She's a sexual being, just like anyone else," Lexie said. "There's nothing wrong with celebrating love."

She ran a finger down the back of his neck. She was pretty sure that sexual energy was responsible for sparking her creativity. And she wanted more. "I bought something from the same shop," she added in a lilting voice. "Aren't you curious?"

"You had a phone call while you were gone," he said. "I let the machine pick it up."

Removing her arms, she wandered over to the blinking machine to check her messages. Recognizing the number, she said, "Good, the gallery called."

She rang Samuel back and while she waited for him to pick up she glanced outside at the angle of the sunlight shining through the studio windows. Perfect.

"Hello, Manyung Gallery."

"Hey, Samuel, Lexie here. You rang?"

"I called about the paintings you have on display. Some of them have been here a couple of months and they're not moving. With the economic downturn and the tourist season coming to an end, you might want to think about lowering the price."

"I can't afford to take less," Lexie said. "Give them a little longer." She hid her worry, remaining calm but firm. "In fact, once the Archibald is over I might be raising the price."

"Okay," Samuel said doubtfully. "I'll give them another few weeks then we'll rethink."

Lexie hung up. Tugging on her hair, she paced the living room. Those paintings were her bread and butter. If they didn't sell…

Rafe cleared his throat. "It's none of my business but since you're going to need money to pay taxes

I'll ask. What was that all about? Do I understand you've got paintings for sale at a gallery?"

Lexie collapsed into a chair at the table and explained the situation. How she sold seascapes at the Manyung Gallery for two to three thousand dollars apiece. "I can usually count on selling at least one a month, sometimes more. But it's been a bad year."

"You don't think you should have lowered the price?" Rafe asked. "A bird in the hand, and all that."

"I need the money to pay my taxes. It's that simple." She thought for a moment. "Maybe I'm not charging enough. People value things when they're expensive." She picked up the phone and called Samuel back. "Forget about waiting until after the Archibald, I'm raising my price right now by ten percent."

"Lexie, are you sure?" Samuel said alarmed. "I don't think—"

"You'll get a bigger cut, too, so don't complain," Lexie said. "I'll bet you a bottle of pinot noir you sell something this weekend."

She clicked off the phone. Part of her enjoyed the buzz of holding her own in the business world. But getting aggressive wasn't good for the creative process.

"Aren't you worried?" Rafe asked. "You don't have a steady income."

"I'm scraping by." She didn't want to think about

the money she owed in taxes. The Archibald Prize—
if she won it—would cover that. If she didn't win she
would find the money, somehow. She would paint
ten trillion watercolors of the colorful huts on Summerside Beach for the local galleries and cafés. She
would paint portraits of pampered Pekinese pooches
for rich old ladies. She would paint kids' faces at
birthday parties.

Closing her eyes, she breathed slowly and deeply
for three counts, allowing her hard edges to dissolve
before she went out to paint. When she opened her
eyes again, Rafe was watching her. "What?"

He hesitated. "Those paintings you've already sold
at the local gallery. I'm going to need the records for
those going back five years."

Her and her big mouth.

"They're all in the envelopes." She twisted her
fingers through the folds of her skirt.

He scrolled through the pages of his computer
spreadsheet, looking at those entries. "Then how
come the most you've been paid for a painting is
one thousand dollars?"

"Samuel pays me the rest in cash," she mum-
bled.

His jaw dropped. Then he slammed a hand flat on
the table, making her jump and the receipts flutter.
"That is frickin' tax evasion. Don't you get it? It's
against the law."

"I'm sorry." She shrugged unhappily. "It's just, if

I go back to teaching, I can't paint. We're not talking millions in corporate tax fraud here. You see how I live. It's not as if I'm getting rich off what I do. I barely make enough to keep myself in art supplies."

"That's not the point."

She bowed her head. "I know."

"I don't enjoy squeezing blood out of a stone but I have to do my job." His hands fisted atop his thighs. "I've already had one notice at work. If I screw up on your audit, that'll be two warnings. Care to guess what happens after three?"

"What did you do the other time?"

"It doesn't matter."

"I'm interested."

"I turned a blind eye to the blackmarket income of a woman who was supporting her sick son and his three children. She was a genuine hard-luck case. But what I did was wrong." He stared her in the eye to make sure she understood the gravity of his situation. "I can't afford to lose my job."

"Sounds like your job is horrible." Having had enough of this conversation, she wandered into the living room, plopped down on the couch and picked up her sketch pad. Flipped it to a fresh page.

Rafe resumed sorting receipts and entering data. After a moment, he said, "I need to stay employed until I can start my own fishing boat charter."

"Really? That's so cool. I didn't think you were

the type to be happy as an accountant for the rest of your life." She began to draw his hands. "When are you going to buy a boat?"

"Someday." He tossed an empty envelope aside.

"Someday?" Her pencil stilled. "That's not good enough. What are you waiting for?"

"A little thing called money. Heard of it? I have to save enough for the deposit, for one thing, so the interest rates don't kill me. And I want a good chunk of money in the bank for a safety net."

"You don't need a safety net," she scoffed, studying his wrists. "You just have to take the leap. Look at me."

"Yes…look at you. Anyway, I've got the boat I want all picked out." Now there was an excitement in his voice that made him seem even younger than his years. He moved around the table to his laptop and quickly brought up a webpage. He spun the computer around so she could see. "That's my dream boat."

"Why don't you take out a loan and buy it?" Lexie asked, glancing at the screen from where she sat. He didn't reply, just gazed at the boat on the website.

Lexie quickly sketched a fishing rod in Rafe's hand on her page, the other hand she had turning the reel.

"My father never got to fulfill his dreams," Rafe said finally, obscurely. He shut down the website and went back to sorting.

"What did he want?" At the end of the line, being pulled from the water, she drew a fish.

"What? Oh. To join the merchant marine, to become a captain eventually," Rafe explained. "He got his seaman's papers when he was nineteen. Then my mum got pregnant. Dad went to work on the docks instead. It was supposed to be temporary, just until I was born and he knew my mum was okay."

Lexie paused drawing to look at Rafe's profile. His bottom lip was caught between his teeth. "What happened?"

Rafe took a moment. "One day they were loading containers onto a ship when the crane cable broke. Dad was pinned, his legs crushed by the container." He shrugged. "The merchant marine doesn't take paraplegics."

"Rafe, I'm sorry."

He swivelled to face her directly. "It's not that easy to take leaps of faith. I need to find the right location, get the financing…."

"You've got a good job. You should talk to my sister. She's the loans manager at Community Bank."

"If I were to start a business, I'd have to quit my job. I'm not sure if the bank would lend to me under those circumstances."

"You won't know unless you try. Why wait another year?" she urged. "Do it now."

His face closed down. "How about those records of sales from the gallery?"

RAFE STOOD at the edge of the deck overlooking Brett O'Connor's huge backyard and wondered how the hell he'd ended up at Lexie's family barbecue. At five-thirty he'd returned to his bed and breakfast and changed out of his suit into jeans and a T-shirt. He'd taken Murphy for a walk and then put him back in the yard at the B&B. Then he'd started walking into the village for a meal at the pub.

Hetty had driven by and stopped right in the middle of the road, blocking traffic, to offer him a lift. His mistake had been getting into her car.

Now he had a frosty bottle of beer in his hand and was standing on the sidelines exchanging a few words with a rugged blond athlete who turned out to be Brett O'Connor, the famous ex-football player. Rafe estimated about fifty guests were gathered for the pre-wedding send-off and celebration. They milled about the yard or sat on the deck. The grill was sizzling with prawns and steaks, and an assortment of salads was laid out on tables.

He had to admit, a backyard barbecue beat a lonely meal in a pub.

A passel of young kids romped on the grass with the dogs—a golden retriever and a Jack Russell terrier. A teenage boy and his girlfriend, both blond and about fourteen years old, sat at the picnic table and talked, holding hands.

Lexie came outside, carrying a platter of raw vegetables to the barbecue. Her hair flowed and curled over her bare shoulders. Her sundress, tiny pink flowers on a turquoise background, molded to her slender curves. As she made her way across the patio he watched her interact with her family and friends. Everyone clearly adored her, even if they thought she was a ditz.

Hetty touched her arm and pointed in his direction. Lexie looked up. There was a moment of stillness when their eyes met. He saw the surprise followed by—

Was that a smile?

Then Brett was saying something to him. "Sorry," Rafe said, dragging his gaze away from Lexie. "I missed that."

"I asked if you wanted to join me in throwing the football around with the kids." Brett tossed the oval ball lightly between his hands.

"Maybe later. I should speak to Lexie." He walked to meet her, stopping in the shade of a pergola thick with grape vines. "I swear to God, your mother kidnapped me."

"Yeah, right." She shook her head but she was definitely smiling. "Couldn't stay away from me, could you? Sienna!" Lexie called, waving to a woman with long curling red hair in a pale green linen dress. She came over and Lexie introduced Rafe. "My sister-in-law to be."

"Pleased to meet you," Rafe said. "I'm impressed by how well Lexie's captured your likeness." And then damned if his gaze didn't drop to her right breast. He quickly looked back up, red-faced.

To his relief, Sienna laughed. "Don't worry," she said drily, "you're not the first to do that." She nodded to Lexie. "How did you go with finding a model of DNA? I've got a biochemistry textbook you can borrow if you like."

"Thanks, but I got what I needed from the internet."

"Good." Sienna waved at an older couple who'd just arrived. "Excuse me. My parents are here. I'll catch up with you later. Nice to meet you, Rafe."

"Likewise." Rafe turned to Lexie. "DNA?"

"I don't understand how it works, but structurally, it's very elegant. Great backdrop for Sienna's portrait."

Hetty came back out of the house bearing the crystal punch bowl brimming with sangria.

"I think your advice to Mum must be working," Lexie said. "When my dad arrived he had the biggest grin you've ever seen."

Rafe sipped his beer and glanced around. "I just hope no one else decides I'm some sort of sex counselor and asks for my services."

"Hey, Lexie," said a woman behind them. The baby girl in her arms gurgled a laugh.

"Sally. And little Chloe!" Lexie embraced both woman and baby. "I'm glad you could make it."

Rafe judged Sally, dressed in jeans and a white top, to be in her early thirties. As for Chloe, he didn't have a clue how old she was. She was young enough to wear knitted booties instead of shoes but old enough to hold her head up by herself. She had big hazel eyes, rosy cheeks and wisps of light brown hair.

Over her shoulder Sally carried a tote bag bristling with baby paraphernalia. Judging by the amount of gear she carried, she was planning to stay for a week.

"This is Rafe," said Lexie, "from the Australian Taxation Office."

"Hi, Rafe." Sally chucked Chloe under the chin. "Can you say hello to Lexie and Rafe?"

Chloe cooed at Lexie and then gave the big bad tax man the once-over. A tiny frown pulled her tiny brows together and her tiny bottom lip came out.

Rafe took a pull of his beer. *The feeling's mutual, kid.*

"Do you want a bottle of mineral water?" Lexie asked Sally. "I'm just on my way back inside."

"I'll come, too. I need to use the bathroom." She glanced around. "Maybe someone will hold Chloe for me."

"Rafe, would you? Just for a few minutes?" Lexie asked.

"I'm not good with babies." Involuntarily, he backed up a step. "She doesn't know me."

"That's okay," Sally said. "I have to go back to work soon so I'm trying to get her get used to going to strangers. Don't worry. She won't bite." Taking no notice of his objections, she handed over the wriggling mess of chubby limbs and drool. "I'll be right back."

Lexie and Sally linked arms and walked off, talking a mile a minute.

Rafe tried to get a grip on Chloe but she was as slippery as she was heavy. Pushing her feet against his stomach, she launched herself after her departing mother. Rafe grunted and grabbed her just before she fell. Then she tried to squirm out of his grasp, slipping as far down as his knee until he was holding her by the collar of her one-piece romper.

Chloe started to cry. Really cry. Loud wails, red cheeks and spurting eyes. In between howls she paused briefly to gulp air and glare at him.

Rafe glanced around for help. The men were chucking a football around with the kids and the women were looking at him with gooey smiles on their faces.

"Chloe, sweetie, what's wrong?" Sally came out on the run, arms outstretched, followed by Lexie. "Is she okay?"

"Here, take her," Rafe said, all but throwing the kid back into her mother's arms.

"It's time for your bottle," Sally crooned to her distraught daughter. She glanced up at Rafe. "What did you do?"

"Nothing!" Rafe held his hands up, palms out. "She's the one who has issues."

Chloe collapsed against her mother's shoulder. Sally carried her over to a lawn chair.

"Don't ever do that to me again," Rafe said to Lexie.

"You were cute with her," Lexie said.

"I don't like kids."

"Don't say that," Lexie protested. "Children are one of the greatest joys in life."

"You don't have any," he pointed out.

Beneath her lightly tanned complexion she paled.

Immediately he regretted his words. Women, especially at Lexie's age, could be sensitive about that sort of thing.

"Sorry. I don't know your story. Maybe there's a reason...you haven't found the right guy or maybe you can't—" He broke off, aware he was putting his foot farther in his mouth.

"I'm not destined to have children," Lexie said quietly.

That was pretty dramatic. What did she even mean by it? Was she infertile? Seeing the way she was around kids, it was impossible to believe she didn't want her own.

"Gather around, everyone." Steve stood on an up-turned plastic milk carton, tapping a spoon against a beer bottle. "Jack's asked me to say a few words. Lexie, Renita, could you come to the front, please."

"Excuse me," Lexie said to Rafe. "Could you hold my glass for me?"

Lexie edged her way through the throng to join her sister. She touched Renita on the arm and they exchanged a smile that needed no words. Their beloved brother was getting married to a woman they already loved like another sister. Yet as Lexie listened to her father, her happiness for the couple was tinged with sadness and, if she was honest, a touch of envy. The conversation just now with Rafe hadn't helped.

As her father conducted a last-minute consultation with Jack and Sienna, Lexie's gaze drifted over the assembled guests. Sienna's father was a tall, distin-guished-looking man with gray hair while her mother appeared reserved with her severe glasses and her wavy red hair chopped short.

Next to them stood a spare, balding man support-ing a frail woman and a sleeping baby. Blue veins were faintly visible in the pale skin of the baby's temples. The child's closed eyelids were transparent and the tiny nose looked carved out of wax.

Lexie nudged Renita. "Who's that?"

"Sienna's ex-husband, Anthony, and his new wife, Erica," Renita replied.

"That's right. Erica had complications, pre-eclampsia or something. Had to deliver. The baby was a preemie. Poor sweet thing." Lexie couldn't drag her eyes away. The baby looked so fragile in her mother's arms. "How premature was she again?"

"Two-and-a-half months, I think." Renita frowned, seeing Lexie's face. "Hey, what's wrong?"

"Nothing. I'm fine. It's just… It must have been so scary for them." She shivered and mustered a smile. "But they're good now. I'm sure the baby will have a bright future."

She glanced over her shoulder, searching out Rafe. She spotted him off to her right, standing next to Brett, talking quietly. He seemed to be having a good time, despite having Chloe foisted on him earlier.

Renita nudged her and nodded toward Sienna and Jack. "What's going on here? This is starting to look like a wedding ceremony."

Lexie blinked. "Last I heard, they were getting married in Bali. But you're right—Sienna even has flowers."

The bridal party, if that's what it was, was forming a semicircle facing the guests. Hetty took her place on Steve's right. The engaged couple stood to his left, with Sienna's son, Oliver, and her parents next to them. Sienna held a bouquet of red roses against her pale green dress. Jack, in a white shirt that showed off his tan, took her hand and they exchanged a smile. There was a distinct buzz in the atmosphere, a sense of anticipation.

"Don't they look gorgeous together?" Lexie whispered to Renita. "And how about Dad? I'm so proud of him for having the guts to speak in front of a crowd."

"Especially after that disastrous speech he made at his and Mum's wedding anniversary." Renita tilted her chin at a well-dressed woman of around fifty with highlighted blond hair edging her way through the ring of assembled guests. "Isn't that the woman we met at Toastmasters when we went to see Dad give his Icebreaker speech?"

"Susan Dwyer, Dad's *friend*. It is, too," Lexie said. "Look at Mother glaring at her. What's she doing as part of the family group? We're not even up there."

"Lady friend?" Renita said sharply.

"Mum seems to think so—" Lexie broke off as Steve cleared his throat in preparation. "I'll tell you later."

Steve adjusted his glasses and glanced at the cards in his hand. He cleared his throat again, smiled nervously. "Thank you all for coming this evening to help celebrate Jack and Sienna's up-coming nuptials." He spoke too fast, running the words together.

The blond woman made a discreet signal with her hand. Yep, she's the one from Toastmasters, Lexie thought; she was coaching him.

Steve continued to speak at a slightly more lei-surely pace. "I'd like to welcome Sienna's parents, Barbara and Neil, who've taken leave from their work at the Mayo Clinic for this special occasion." There was a brief round of applause before Steve continued, "I couldn't ask for a more wonderful daughter-in-law. And having a doctor in the family will be handy."

He glanced at Sienna's parents with a smile. "Make that three doctors." Everyone chuckled. "I'd also like to welcome Sienna's son, Oliver, to the family."

The boy blushed to the roots of his thick blond hair.

Lexie saw Hetty smile up at Steve, conveying her support. But Steve was looking to Susan Dwyer for approval. Hetty followed the direction of his gaze and her smile faded. *Uh-oh,* Lexie thought.

"As you all know, Jack and Sienna planned a small private wedding ceremony in Bali, preceded by this reception," Steve went on. "A few weeks ago Jack came to me and said they changed their minds. When they travel to Bali in a few days' time it will be for a honeymoon, as husband and wife. Tonight, in front of their family and friends, they will exchange wedding vows."

Startled gasps went up from the crowd.

"Did you know about this?" Lexie asked Renita.

"No! I can't believe they didn't tell us."

"Now I'd like to introduce Susan Dwyer," Steve said as the blonde stepped forward. "As well as an accomplished Toastmaster, Susan is a marriage celebrant."

Calling Jack and Sienna forward, Susan conducted a brief but moving ceremony. Then Jack and Sienna faced each other, hands clasped between them, and took turns speaking heartfelt vows. The throb of emotion in their voices brought a lump to Lexie's throat. Jack's fingers trembled as he slid a gold band on Sienna's hand. And Sienna's tremulous smile as she gazed up at him was one of absolute love. She lifted her face to be kissed and Jack's arms went around her.

Lucky, lucky couple to have found each other. Lexie brushed away a tear. When she glanced up she saw Rafe watching her. His expression was unreadable. Did he think this was all too romantic and sentimental? He'd better not. Jack and Sienna had both been through difficulties and deserved a second shot at marital happiness.

With the ceremony over, the guests erupted in cheers and clapping. Sienna and Jack broke apart with wide smiles. Steve called for all the unattached women to come forward as Jack stepped back and Sienna prepared to throw her bouquet.

"Go on, Lexie," Renita said, giving her sister a gentle shove. "And don't give me that 'married to your art' rubbish. It's about time you hooked up with someone. Mum let it slip about you and Rafe. He's hot, I'll give you that. But you always pick guys you would never marry."

"I do not," Lexie protested. "Anyway, catching a bunch of flowers won't lead me to the man of my dreams, if he even exists. I'm not going up there. I'd feel silly. Let the young women and the girls take part."

"Young women? You're not old."

She felt old today. Her younger brother had just gotten married for the second time. Renita and Brett were going to tie the knot in the not too distant future. Her longest relationship had lasted two years and that had been with a man who'd been on the rebound. She'd helped him heal and then he'd met someone else and moved on. As she'd always known he would. Other than him, there'd been guys who were about to move overseas, guys who were commitment-phobes, guys she liked but didn't love.

Now she'd hooked up with Rafe. Temporarily.

Could Renita possibly be right?

Sienna was calling her, refusing to throw her bouquet until Lexie came to the front. The rest of the unmarried women included Brett's thirteen-year-old daughter, Tegan, and a handful of women in their twenties. The audience started slow-clapping.

"They won't stop until you go," Renita said.

"This is embarrassing," Lexie muttered. Did everyone see her as an old maid who needed all the help she could get to find a husband? But Renita was right. The only way to make it stop was to get this over with. She shook out her hair and then stepped to the front.

A cheer went up from the well-lubricated crowd. Sienna turned her back to the women and with a big two-handed toss, threw her roses over her head. Lexie stepped back to where she should have been out of range. But Sienna had a strong arm. The bouquet sailed over Tegan's head, bounced off another woman's shoulder and landed in Lexie's arms.

Lexie buried her nose in the fragrant flowers to hide the sudden unexpected welling of tears in her eyes. She didn't believe in marriage and happily ever after and all the claptrap. At least not for her. So it was ridiculous to cry just because she'd caught the bridal bouquet.

Blinking, she raised her head and laughed, so no one would know she'd been so close to tears.

CHAPTER SEVEN

"WHAT DO YOU THINK?" Lexie made another twirl around Rafe in her petal-pink silk camisole with lacy push-up bra and matching thong.

They'd come back to her place after the barbecue. Rafe still wore his polo shirt and jeans, but Lexie had changed, eager to show off her new garment.

His eyes blazed. "I think you're beautiful. And hot."

She stroked her hands down her breasts to her hips. "I don't usually go in for sexy lingerie but I couldn't resist. The silk feels so soft against my skin. Here, you feel."

He placed his hands on her hips and his fingers branded her through the thin fabric, as if the silk itself had dissolved from his heat. "Is your mother coming back here tonight?"

"No. She decided it wasn't a good idea to leave my dad alone. I don't think Dad's interested in that woman but I can see why it bothers Mum." She went up on tiptoe and began to kiss him, unbuttoning his shirt. He shut his eyes as she slid a leg up the inside of his thigh. "Let's go outside. In the moonlight."

His eyes snapped open. "Outside?"

Lexie pushed away from him and picked up a throw rug from the couch. She tossed it to him and grabbed another, swirling it around her like a cape. "Come on."

The full moon rode high in a starless sky, bathing trees and houses in silvery light and glinting off the koi pond beneath the camellia tree. The night air was cool on her skin, but pleasantly so. A brushy-tail possum scampered across the electrical wire leading from the house to the studio, thudded across the roof and crashed through the trees along the creek.

It was only as Lexie hoisted herself onto the trampoline that she realized Rafe hadn't followed her. She spread the rug. Where was he?

The back door swung open. Rafe—clad only in his boxers—appeared with a pillow under his arm, a bottle of champagne and two flutes in his hands, the rug slung around his neck.

"Where did this come from?" she asked, taking the bottle and glasses from him so he could climb up.

"I bought it yesterday and stuck it in the back of your fridge." He placed the pillow so she could lean against it and popped the cork, spilling the foaming liquid into the flutes.

Lexie raised her glass. "To living for pleasure."

"I'll drink to that," Rafe said, and they clinked. He glanced around at the fence blocking the view from the street, the high hedge separating her yard from her neighbors, and the studio and tall gum trees at the back of the lot, bordering the creek. "Do you make love out here often?"

"First time." She sipped the bubbly wine. "But I've always wanted to."

He leaned down to kiss her, the taste of champagne on his tongue. She shivered and he pulled back, taking her glass and the bottle and wedging them between the springs. Then he lay down beside her and drew her to him in a long searching kiss. Their bodies moved together. Springs creaking, the cool rubber mat of the trampoline bounced lightly beneath their weight as they shifted positions.

She laughed with the strangeness of it and he rolled her suddenly, chuckling as their odd mattress sprang back and her eyes widened. Then he stilled and the trampoline dipped in the center forcing them closer. Rafe's arms went around her, his legs twined with hers. She could feel him hard and pulsing against the moist warm silk of her lingerie. Her blood began to throb.

He eased out of the kiss, his lips a whisper away from hers. His long lashes were individual spikes of black as his eyes met hers. "I'm twenty-six years old. I just wondered if you knew."

Twenty-six.

He was even younger than she'd thought. She was nearly forty. He was just a baby.

"How would I?" She gave a breathy laugh and ran a finger over the rasp of dark stubble on his chin. "Do you…know how old I am?"

"I saw your birth date on one of your documents." A second later, he added, "You look amazing."

For your age. Lexie rolled onto her back. She should congratulate herself on attracting a hot young guy. Small recompense.

"I'm really robbing the cradle, aren't I?"

"I like to think I'm a grown man."

"You're not worried because I caught the bouquet, are you?" Lexie asked suddenly. "Everyone seems to think I want to get married but it doesn't mean I do. It doesn't mean *I* think you're the one."

"No, that would be crazy. We hardly know each other. We're so…different." He gazed up at the moon. "By noon tomorrow I'll have finished tabulating the raw data. In the afternoon I'll prepare a tax assessment for you. Tomorrow evening I'll leave Summerside and finish the audit at the office next week."

Studying his long forehead and straight nose in profile she felt a pang of regret…envy…for how young and handsome he was.

"So, one more night together." She pressed against him. "How are we going to make the most of it?"

Rafe inserted a finger under the flat silk strap of her chemise and slid it down her bare arm. He kissed the spot on her shoulder where it had been, then trailed more kisses down her breast. "I've got some ideas…."

Lexie pushed aside the regret she wasn't supposed to be feeling and moved into his arms. "I'll just bet you do."

RAFE WOKE at dawn and slipped out of Lexie's rumpled bed, leaving her to sleep. He tiptoed down the hall and dressed in the living room. Murphy rose from his makeshift bed of an old blanket, tail wagging, ready for anything.

"Come on, Murph. Let's go fishing. This is probably our last chance."

Rafe walked down the quiet road toward the sea, listening to the birds waking, watching the sky gradually lighten. He stopped in at the bed and breakfast to get his fishing rod and a jacket. The early breeze off the water was chilly.

Rafe kicked at a stone, sending it skittering into the bushes. He turned down Cliff Road and at the cul-de-sac took the trail to the beach. Murphy trotted beside him across the sand, stopping to sniff a dead jellyfish tangled in seaweed. Rafe walked out to the end of the spit of rocks. With a stone he smashed open a mussel and threaded the glistening meat onto his hook for bait. Then he cast his line in a long curving arc, watching it land in the choppy waves offshore.

As he reeled it slowly in, he did some simple

calculations. When he was fifty, she would be sixty-two.

Hmm.

The line emerged from the water dripping as he reeled it in, the hook empty. Crouching on the rock, waves soaking the soles of his sneakers, he replaced the bait and cast again.

His mind drifted to his fishing charter. Why *didn't* he start it sooner rather than later?

Starting a business, being self-employed, was risky. Lexie would be familiar with that. Sure she'd sold a couple of paintings, which combined had a hefty price tag. But looking over her accounts for several years he could see how low her income was in general, and how erratic. The fishing charter business was seasonal. What if he had no money coming in during winter? Boats were money pits.

At a tug on the line, he jerked the rod. He started reeling in, letting out a little, then reeling in again. A fat snapper breached the surface. He broke into a grin. It was moments like this...

EYES CLOSED, Lexie burrowed deeper under the covers. Then she sniffed. Was she imagining things or was that fish frying? She threw the covers back and walked naked down the hall to the kitchen.

Rafe was at the stove, his back to her, flipping a fish fillet. His damp pant legs were rolled up to mid-calf and grains of sand still clung to his bare feet.

"So I wasn't dreaming. There really is a man cooking in my kitchen." She stretched languorously, pushing her hands through her hair.

Rafe turned, did a double take. The piece of fish dropped off his spatula into Murphy's waiting jaws. "Murph, no!" Rafe dropped the spatula, too, as she sauntered over and slid her arms around his neck to nibble on his ear. "That was your fault."

She rubbed her big toe in the sensitive hollow below his ankle. "How can I make it up to you?"

It was ridiculously easy to lure him back to bed, even leaving his fish half-cooked.

She was going to miss this when he was gone.

After they made love Lexie lay on Rafe's chest listening to his heart beating. Memorizing the texture of his skin and the way the dark hair grew in swirls. She lifted her head to see his face. His eyes were open and he was staring at the ceiling. "What are you thinking?"

"That I can't stay in bed all day." A small smile curled his lip. "I have other fish to fry."

She groaned and hit him with a pillow. Then she rolled out of bed and went into the en suite washroom to turn on the shower. She stepped under the spray. A moment later, Rafe opened the shower door. They made love beneath the cascade of warm water. Then he soaped her back before sluicing it off with his hands.

"Your turn," she said, spinning him around. She

smoothed soapy hands over his shoulders and down his back. Then she slipped her arms around his waist. His fingers twined with hers, clasped to his chest. For a moment they stood there, the water beating down, her head resting on his back, his head bowed.

Not speaking. Not thinking. Just…being.

Hell. This could get emotional if they weren't careful.

She eased back and reached to shut off the water. "How about that fish? I'm starving."

They ate fried fish coated in cornmeal, washing it down with herbal tea.

Lexie got up abruptly after breakfast and went out to the studio, leaving the dishes in the sink and Rafe to tackle the last three envelopes and prepare her tax return.

She took her painting smock off a hook and slipped it on. Then she squeezed worms of Viridian Green and Cadmium Yellow onto her palette and mixed them with a bit of ochre.

The familiar smell of oil paint and linseed oil permeated the air as she mixed her colors. With a printed-out picture of the molecular structure of DNA to guide her, Lexie chose a brush with a fine tip and started painting in tiny hexagons. The ghostly genetic material took shape in shades of bronze against a pale green background, a modern foil for Sienna's almost medieval blue robe and wild red hair. It gave the soft romanticism of Sienna's portrait a scientific edge and conveyed the continuity of life through reproduction.

Lexie put down her brush, a catch in her throat. *Stop it.* No reason to get emotional. It wasn't as though she'd had a milestone birthday, like the big four-O. She was only thirty-eight, for goodness sake.

Babies were a nonissue as far as she was concerned. She'd had nearly two decades to get pregnant if she'd wanted to. Why should she feel so upset that it hadn't happened?

"So, THIS IS IT." Lexie wore a determined smile.

"I guess." Rafe transferred his briefcase to his other hand, started to reach out, then gripped the handle with both hands. He'd completed the audit and now he was leaving. End of story.

"In a week or two you'll get a letter from the tax office telling how much you owe, and when and where to pay the bill," he explained.

"A letter from the tax office, or from you?" She straightened his collar, patted down the lapels of his suit. Then she ran a hand through his hair, ruffling it.

"You've got to take this seriously." Rafe captured her hand and held it tightly. "The letter will be from me. If you have any questions, just give me a buzz."

"Okay." She glanced down at the business card he'd given her. "How long will the next part take?"

"A couple of weeks. I have to consult with my supervisor…"

"Over what?" She blinked her big blue eyes, entirely too trusting.

Despite their bedroom antics, he couldn't cheat the tax office for her sake. "How much the fine will be. Have you got any savings?"

"A thousand dollars. Maybe. Why?"

"Because you're going to owe a lot of money," he said. "I'm not sure you understand that."

"I'm not stupid. Don't look so worried." She flapped her hands. "I just can't think about it right now. If anything throws me, I won't be able to paint. And I *have* to focus on my painting."

"Just promise me you won't forget to pay the bill. If you evade that, it will bring down criminal charges."

For the first time, she looked worried. "Criminal charges. I thought you were joking when you told me you could call in the Federal Police."

"This is no joke, Lexie." He glanced away, checking that Murphy hadn't run onto the road, then back at her. "I've got to go if I'm going to beat the rush hour."

She smiled wistfully. "When you buy your boat, I'll paint the name on it for you."

"Deal," he said. The chances of that ever happening were slim to none. If—no, *when*—he bought his boat, he wouldn't be calling her up. She knew it, too.

He kissed her for the last time. And then he left without looking back.

RAFE KNOCKED on Larry's open door. Hearing his boss grunt by way of invitation, he entered. The boxy office held a couple of potted plants, a bank of filing cabinets and credenza displaying Larry's collection of miniature pistol replicas.

Larry was tapping at his computer keyboard with four fingers. He glanced at Rafe over the half-glasses perched on the end of his long nose. "You're back."

"Mission accomplished." Rafe dropped Lexie's thirty-two-page audit on Larry's desk. "She was evading taxes, all right, although not with malicious intent."

Larry leaned back in his chair. "What was the reason?"

Rafe shrugged. "She's poor. Too disorganized to save money. Ditzy as they come. All of the above." He felt bad talking about her like that, as if he was betraying her even though it was all true.

Larry flicked through the stapled sheets, pausing to check a figure here and there, reading over the summation. "I see the total tax payment is $21,390. Plus penalties of $10,000."

Rafe nodded, pressing a hand to his stomach. There was no way she could pay that.

Larry narrowed his eyes at Rafe. "Is this comprehensive? You haven't left anything out?"

"On my honor," Rafe said, moving his hand to cover his heart. "As well as the two paintings the IRS brought to our attention, I found records of thirty-eight lesser works she hadn't declared."

Larry smiled broadly. "Good man! I knew you would come through." He sobered, tapping Rafe's report with his pen. "Of course I'll be checking this thoroughly."

"Get out your fine-tooth comb," Rafe said. "It's legit."

"In that case, congratulations. No more black marks," Larry said. "*And* you'll be eligible for a bonus."

Rafe shut his eyes briefly, relief washing over him. In its wake came a sense of hope. The end of this job was in sight.

Smiling, Rafe backed out of Larry's office. "Thanks, boss."

With a black coffee and a half-eaten hamburger at his elbow, Rafe sat in his cubicle and started to review the file for his next audit, a take-out fish-and-chip restaurant.

He was finding it difficult to concentrate. He was worried, too, for Lexie's sake. How would she pay? She was living off two-minute noodles for cripes' sake. And she was counting on winning the Archibald to get the money to pay her taxes. To his inexpert eye her painting seemed pretty good but how realistic was she being?

He caught himself with a shake of his head. Lexie was just an auditee. Not his problem.

The main thing was, he'd kept his job. With a possible bonus.

He could buy a boat.

He threw down his pen and got to his feet. He paced a few steps away from his cubicle, thinking furiously. Why wait another year? He could live on the boat if he had to.

He dropped back into his chair and quickly pulled up a boat brokering website he had bookmarked. There were three used Steber 47 fishing boats for sale in the greater metropolitan area. He was jotting down phone numbers and addresses when Chris strolled in from lunch sipping from a coffee take-out cup.

"How was your jaunt to the seaside?" Chris put his cup on his desk and removed his glasses to polish them on the hem of his shirt.

Rafe hesitated. He and Chris were the same age and shared a love of fishing and boutique beer. Even though they were friends, Rafe was wary of saying too much about Summerside, especially at the office.

"I went there to work," he said. "Not have fun."

"Who said anything about fun?" Chris said, putting his glasses back on. "You were going down there to nail some artist chick for tax evasion. How did that pan out?"

"She's going to have to pay penalties. As expected." *Actually, I did nail the blonde.*

Chris nodded to the computer screen. "Still drooling over the Steber, huh?"

"I'm going to go look at a couple this weekend," Rafe said. "Want to come?"

"Can't. Laura's mum is looking after Jordon so Laura and I can go away for the weekend. First time alone since the birth." Chris glanced at his watch. "Better get back to work. You'll have to come over for dinner soon. Maybe we'll fix you up with one of Laura's friends."

"Yeah, sure."

He wished he'd taken a photo of Lexie or something. Just to remember her by.

Hang on. He quickly did an internet search for Lexie Thatcher. She had a website displaying her paintings. He clicked through the pages. It didn't look as if she'd updated it for a while— He stopped. There was a photo of her next to one of her seascapes at some gallery. He clicked on it to enlarge it. For some minutes he just looked at her face. And remembered.

IT WAS *good* Rafe was gone, Lexie told herself as she prepared for another day in front of her easel. She'd gotten a lot done in the weeks since he'd left.

Yet, without that fabulous sex she wasn't sleeping as soundly as before. It didn't help that she was putting in long hours at the easel.

This new version of Sienna's portrait was taking longer than she'd anticipated because the DNA structure was so intricate and the area to be covered was large. She wasn't a fast painter and she often painted a section out and started over. So even though she still had a couple of months until the Archibald Prize deadline, she would need every minute.

Rafe's business card was tucked into the corner of the notice board in her studio. There was no reason to call him, not until she got her tax assessment. But she thought about him every day.

"Lexie!" Hetty knocked on the open door. She wore a long blue flowing dress and white clogs. She was holding a white plastic bag. "Are you busy?"

"When I'm in my studio I'm always busy." Lexie despaired of ever convincing her family that what she did was work. She carried on arranging her brushes and oils, deciding which colors to squeeze onto her palette.

"I won't stay long," Hetty said, sweeping in with a rustle of plastic. "I brought you some lemons from our tree." She put the bag on the long trestle table where Lexie framed her larger paintings. "Are you okay? You look pale. You should at least get out for a walk, sweetheart. You never see the sun."

"I'm fine. Thanks for the lemons." Lexie mixed

Get 2 Books FREE!

Harlequin® Books,
publisher of women's fiction,
presents

HARLEQUIN®

Super Romance®

GET 2 BOOKS

We'd like to send you two *Harlequin® Superromance®* novels absolutely fr
Accepting them puts you under no obligation to purchase any more book

HOW TO GET YOUR
2 FREE BOOKS AND 2 FREE GIFTS

1. Return the reply card today, and we'll send you two *Harlequin Superromance* novels, absolutely free! We'll even pay the postage!

2. Accepting free books places you under no obligation to buy anything, ever. Whatever you decide, the free books and gifts are yours to keep, free!

3. We hope that after receiving your free books you'll want to remain a subscriber, but the choice is yours—to continue or cancel, any time at all!

EXTRA BONUS

You'll also get two free mystery gifts! (worth about $10)

FREE!

Return this card today to get
2 FREE BOOKS and 2 FREE GIFTS!

HARLEQUIN®
Super Romance®

YES! Please send me 2 FREE *Harlequin® Superromance®*
novels, and 2 free mystery gifts as well. I understand
I am under no obligation to purchase anything, as
explained on the back of this insert.

*About how many NEW paperback fiction books have
you purchased in the past 3 months?*

❏ 0-2   ❏ 3-6   ❏ 7 or more
E9ND   E9NP   E9NZ

❏ I prefer the regular-print edition   ❏ I prefer the larger-print edition
135/336 HDL   139/339 HDL

FIRST NAME _____ LAST NAME _____

ADDRESS _____

APT.# _____ CITY _____

Visit us at:
www.ReaderService.com

STATE/PROV. _____ ZIP/POSTAL CODE _____

▶ **DETACH AND MAIL CARD TODAY!** ▶

(H-SR-03/11)

If offer card is missing, write to: The Reader Service, P.O. Box 1867, Buffalo, NY 14240-1867 or visit www.ReaderService.com

BUSINESS REPLY MAIL

FIRST-CLASS MAIL   PERMIT NO. 717   BUFFALO, NY

POSTAGE WILL BE PAID BY ADDRESSEE

THE READER SERVICE
PO BOX 1867
BUFFALO NY 14240-9952

NO POSTAGE
NECESSARY
IF MAILED
IN THE
UNITED STATES

more of the bronze color for the sugar hexagons. "Have you heard anything from Jack and Sienna in Bali?"

"No, but I got an email from Oliver." Hetty placed the bag of fruit among the odds and ends of canvases and frames. "He's snorkeling on the coral reef every day."

"That'll give Jack and Sienna plenty of time to themselves," Lexie said.

Hetty peered at the painting. "Is that lace?"

"No, it's a DNA double helix." When Hetty still looked perplexed Lexie gestured with her paintbrush. "Genetics, reproduction, biological clock…?"

"Oh, I see." Hetty hoisted herself onto a high wooden stool and propped her clogs on the rungs. "Have you heard from Rafe?"

"No," Lexie replied, trying not to express her impatience that her mother was still here. "I don't expect to until I get my tax invoice."

"I don't understand how you can be so calm about that."

"Getting upset isn't going to do any good." Lexie wiped her brush with a turpentine-soaked rag and dipped it in another color before resuming her detailed work. "If I win the Archibald then all that energy I spent worrying would have been wasted."

"No, I meant how can you be so calm about not seeing the man? I thought you two hit it off. Now he's just…gone."

Lexie's hand jerked, leaving a blotch of paint on the canvas. She reached for a toothpick to scrape it off. "How's everything with you and Dad?"

"That's why I was hoping Rafe would be here. He gave me such good advice I wanted to ask him what to do about the other woman."

"What can a young man who's practically a stranger tell you about your marriage? Anyway, what other woman? It was obvious at the reception that Susan Dwyer is just Dad's mentor." Lexie threw the toothpick in a bin. "You and he need to fit in with each other's interests. Why don't you ask him to come to one of your meditation retreats?"

"He wouldn't go." Hetty dismissed that with a wave. "He thinks we're a cult or some such foolishness."

"Tell him how important it is to you," she said. "Make him understand that your marriage is at a critical point."

Hetty gazed unhappily at her fingers as she twisted her chunky silver rings. "What if he doesn't love me enough to do that for me?"

"It doesn't seem like a lot to ask," Lexie said gently, "after all the years you've had together."

Hetty was silent a moment. "I wonder sometimes if we have anything together anymore." She slid off the stool and gave Lexie a hug. "I'll see you soon. Take care of yourself."

She left and Lexie went back to her painting. This

malaise, or whatever she was feeling, would pass. But Hetty's parting words lingered. Lexie and Rafe had certainly shared something.

An obsession with each other's bodies.

CHAPTER EIGHT

"WHAT SEEMS to be the problem?" Dr. Natalie Higgins lifted her stethoscope to listen to Lexie's chest. Natalie's straight brown hair was pulled back from her heart-shaped face with a thin black headband, making her look even younger than her thirty-something years.

"I'm tired all the time," Lexie said. "I can hardly drag myself out of bed in the morning."

When Rafe had been around, both her energy and her creativity had been flowing full throttle. He'd been gone for four weeks now and she'd become increasingly lethargic.

Natalie lowered her stethoscope. "Rest your arm on the desk, please."

Lexie planted her forearm next to a framed photo of Natalie's smiling two-year-old daughter. "How's Millie?" she asked, nodding at the picture. Lexie remembered when Natalie had married Deepra, the local pathologist, five years ago. She'd rejoiced with her GP when Natalie had gotten pregnant and had followed Millie's progress through every stage.

"She's toilet trained," Natalie said proudly as she

strapped the blood pressure cuff onto Lexie's arm. "One day she just decided she'd had enough of diapers and within a week she was using the toilet."

"That's great," Lexie said. "She's so cute."

"Your heart sounds fine. Your blood pressure's good," Natalie said, hanging up the cuff. "I'll order some blood work. You might be low on iron. Are you run-down for any reason?"

"I've been working hard for months to get a portrait finished for the Archibald."

Natalie wrote out a lab request for blood tests. "Is that stressful?"

"Yes," Lexie admitted. "I'm happy with what I'm doing now but it's touch and go whether I'll get it done in time. The deadline is in ten days."

"How are your periods? Are they regular? Flow not too heavy?" Natalie started scanning through Lexie's records on the computer.

"Um. I think so. I can't remember."

Natalie's hands stilled on the keys. "Could you be pregnant?"

"No, no. I have an IUD. Dr. Klein put it in a couple of years ago."

Natalie slanted her a glance. "You've been seeing me for six years. Hang on while I finish looking at your notes." She clicked back through computer pages.

Lexie waited patiently. Sienna worked here now, too, and Lexie saw her if she had something simple like a sinus infection, but she didn't feel comfortable getting undressed in front of her sister-in-law.

"It's been longer than a couple of years," Natalie said. "More like ten. IUDs should be replaced every five years or so. Would you like me to do that now?"

"Ten years," Lexie murmured. How had the time gone so quickly? "Sure, might as well while I'm here."

"IUDs aren't generally inserted in women who haven't had a baby." Natalie rose and opened a cabinet full of medical supplies to look for an IUD. "Have you had a child?"

The room was silent but for the quiet clink of metal as Natalie readied her instruments.

"N-no."

"Was there a reason you went with an IUD?" Natalie asked, tearing into the packaging.

"I—I didn't want to have to worry about remembering to take a pill," Lexie went on. "Dr. Klein said it would be fine."

"You haven't had any problems with it?"

"No."

"Okay. Undress from the waist down and hop up on the bed beneath the sheet." Natalie drew the curtains. "Let me know when you're ready."

On the wall next to the bed was a poster depicting the cross-section of a woman twelve weeks' pregnant. Lexie studied it as she undressed even though she knew by heart that at that stage of development the toes and fingers were formed, the fingernails were beginning to grow and, although the mother couldn't feel it, the baby was kicking his tiny legs and clenching and unclenching his fists.

She set her folded clothes on the chair and lay beneath the sheet. "I'm ready."

Natalie pulled back the curtain, her manner brisk. She drew on a pair of gloves, got Lexie to position her legs. "I'm going to do an internal examination. It might feel a bit uncomfortable. Just try to relax." After a few minutes of gentle probing she said, "Have you felt the strings of your IUD lately?"

"I don't take much notice of it. Sometimes they get stuck inside."

"When did you say your last period was?"

"I can't remember. It's been a while. I must be due for one."

"That's odd." Natalie tilted her face up to the ceiling as she gently probed farther.

Lexie breathed slow, calming breaths, taking herself to the bottom of the still pond.

"I can't locate the strings at all." Natalie pulled the gooseneck lamp down and inserted the speculum. She worked in silence for a few more minutes. Then she removed the instrument, pushed away the lamp and pulled off her disposable gloves.

"What is it?" Lexie said. "Is everything all right?"

Natalie moved to the supply cabinet and dropped

her instruments in disinfectant. "Your IUD must have fallen out. It can happen without a woman even noticing."

Lexie propped herself up on her elbows. "H-how long?"

"It's impossible to tell." Natalie returned to the bedside and folded her small hands over her dark pants. "But by the looks of things, I'd say at least four weeks."

Lexie flopped back down and closed her eyes. "I—I've been sexually active."

"I thought you might have," Natalie said.

Lexie's eyes snapped open. She gripped the sheet between her fingers, crushing it. "What do you mean?"

"You're pregnant."

Her mouth opened but no sound came out. Then she groaned. Of all the stupid things—

"I take it this isn't a happy discovery." Natalie reached for Lexie's hand. "Are you in a relationship?"

Lexie shook her head. *What was she going to do?*

"Do you know who the father is?" Natalie probed gently.

"Yes." She clenched her teeth as Rafe's image flashed before her. "But he's only twenty-six. He's got plans for his life that don't include children. He doesn't even *like* kids."

"You'll need to tell him," Natalie counseled, still holding Lexie's hand. "But if you don't want to carry the baby to term you have the option to—"

"No." Lexie lurched to a sitting position, tugging her hand free. "I will not abort this baby."

Natalie's brown eyes widened slightly. "I can see you feel strongly. Is there anything you want to talk about? As a doctor or—" her voice softened "—as a friend."

Lexie leaned back on the pillow. "No. But thank you."

"There's also adoption," Natalie suggested. "You wouldn't have any trouble finding a good home for your child."

"I couldn't give my baby away." Just the thought of someone else bringing up her little boy or girl was enough to bring tears to her eyes. But then, tears were always close to the surface these days. At least now she knew the cause was probably hormones.

"Many women nowadays bring up children on their own," Natalie said. "I've gathered from things you've told me in the past that you love children. Maybe you can come to see this in a positive light."

"I do love children but—" She just didn't deserve to have one. "It's…complicated." Lexie hiccupped on a sob.

Natalie patted her hand and rose to draw the curtain. "Everything will work out. You'll see."

Lexie managed a smile.

But she knew in her heart that Natalie was wrong.

RAFE'S RUBBER-SOLED SHOES sounded dully on the wooden wharf at Mordialloc's tidal inlet, half an hour up the coast road from Summerside. Palm trees cast long thin shadows. Waves lapped at the pilings and the smell of salt and diesel came up from the oily water below.

A heat wave had thrown them back into summer and above the water the air shimmered. His shirt was sticking to him as he wiped his forehead, searching out the fishing boat for sale.

Ah, there it was, at the end of the pontoon. The For Sale sign was propped in the port of the main cabin. The vessel was fifty feet long, painted white with an aqua-blue stripe below the gunnel, and a flying bridge.

It looked perfect, big enough to handle a weekend charter chasing tuna and mackerel on the open ocean. But small enough to take day fishers out on the bay to catch flathead and snapper. He could see himself sitting on his deck at the end of the day with a beer, watching the sun set over the water. At night, the waves lapping at the hull would lull him to sleep.

He figured he needed to work at the tax office another year. He would run fishing charters on week-ends and build his business up before he was ready to take the plunge and fish full-time.

A stocky, weathered man wearing a navy fisherman's cap over his gray hair came out of the cabin onto the deck. His faded blue T-shirt hung untucked. "G'day, mate. You looking for something?"

"Are you the owner?" Rafe walked down the narrow pontoon between berths and extended a hand. "I called this morning. Rafe Ellersley."

"Dom Costopolous." He shook Rafe's hand then gestured to the mounting block on the wharf. "Come aboard. Welcome."

Rafe climbed up and over the rail onto the large flat back deck. He noted the coolers, hoses for washing, the twin diesel engines, then glanced back to Dom, who regarded him with piercing black eyes.

"What do you think?" Dom said. "She's a beautiful boat."

Rafe kept his poker face in place. Thank goodness Dom couldn't see how fast his heart was beating. Over the past two weekends he'd looked at three other boats. This one was fifteen years old and a bit worn, but it was in the best condition, by far. With a new paint job and covers on the seating, it would be just fine.

"Can I take a look inside?"

"Of course." Dom smiled and gestured. "Be my guest."

They stepped over the threshold into the main cabin. Rafe took in the eating area, the galley and a settee. Off to his left were tucked a couple of bunks. "How many does it sleep?"

"Eight comfortably. Ten in a pinch." He opened a narrow door. "In here's the head, complete with a shower. The handle on the toilet is a bit sticky but it works. Everything works." Wheezing a little, he moved on. "More bunks up forward. Back here's the captain's cabin. Come, now we go to the flying bridge."

Dom led the way back outside and up the gangway to the control center of the boat. There was radar, depth sounder, fish finder…everything Rafe was looking for.

"Did you use it as a fishing charter?" Rafe asked.

"Yep." Dom took a blue handkerchief from his back pocket and wiped his nose. "I'm too old now to fish. I want to sit in my backyard and drink wine and play with my grandchildren. My sons, they're not interested." He shrugged, palms upraised. "What are you going to do?"

"How old are the engines?" Rafe asked. "Is the servicing up-to-date?"

"Practically brand new," Dom told him. "Two years ago I replaced both of them. I've got all the service records. I'll show you later. Right now we'll take her for a spin. Okay?"

Rafe grinned. "You bet."

With the turn of a key, Dom started the powerful

engines. Rafe felt the throb of the motor right through his breastbone.

"You want to cast off?" Dom said.

"Sure." Rafe descended to the deck, sliding both hands down the handrails, his shoes barely touching the rungs of the gangway. He leaped onto the dock, lifted the thick looped lines off the bollards and sprang aboard as Dom slowly pulled away.

Back on the flying bridge Dom was chewing a toothpick between his back molars. "It's not easy to get a permanent berth in the marina, eh? If you buy the boat, you can take over the lease."

Rafe nodded noncommittally as Dom chugged slowly through the marina's narrow waterway lined with sailboats and fishing boats. They passed beneath the bridge into the mouth of Mordialloc harbor.

On the depth sounder Dom pointed out the shifting bar of sand at the entrance. "You gotta look out for the current on the ebbing tide." He pushed the throttle forward, increasing speed as they headed into open water. "You buy my boat, I'll show you the best fishing spots in the whole bay."

Rafe just smiled and shrugged. He'd believe that if it happened. But if the old geezer was on the level…

When they were clear of small craft traffic Dom glanced at Rafe. "You wanna take the wheel, see how she handles?"

Standing with his feet planted wide, Rafe opened

the boat right up. He could feel the thrum of the motor. The wind blew his hair off his face. Gulls wheeled up and away from them. His grin spread till his cheeks felt sore. So much for a poker face. He turned the boat in a wide circle, the hull bouncing over the choppy waves. On the shore people were sunbathing and swimming in the shallows.

After a good twenty minutes putting the boat through its paces, Dom guided the fishing vessel into the marina and up to the dock. Rafe jumped off and hauled on the lines, pulling the boat in close before tying it off on the bollards.

Back on board, Dom brought all the documentation associated with the vessel to the table in the main cabin. "You look," he said, showing Rafe the engine specifications and maintenance records. "Then we talk."

Rafe studied the papers. Everything seemed to be in order. He glanced up at the older man. "It's more than I wanted to pay. Are you willing to negotiate?"

Dom gave an elaborate shrug. "Maybe I can drop a little. But not much."

Despite his easygoing nature, the fisherman drove a hard bargain. Rafe had to be cagey, too. He'd been to the bank and they were willing to lend him only so much money. He'd cashed in his term deposits to raise the money for the down payment.

After going back and forth, Rafe finally said, "I

want the boat." He named a figure. "That is what I can spend."

Dom planted his elbows on the table, his jaw out-thrust as he pondered the matter. He named another figure. They went back and forth a few more times.

Finally Rafe leaned back. "That's my last offer. I can't do any more."

Dom nodded, looked up at Rafe, and then held out a callused hand. "It's a deal."

Grinning, Rafe pumped his hand. "Anytime you want, you can come fishing with me."

"We drink to that!" Dom slapped the table. He went to the galley and brought out a bottle of ouzo and two small glasses. He poured them each a shot. Holding his aloft, he said, "To the good fishing."

"To fishing!" Rafe clinked glasses and drank. The sharp licorice-flavored liqueur burned down his throat.

Dom immediately poured another shot. He pushed aside the engine maintenance records and brought out a navigation chart of the waters of Port Phillip Bay. With a gleaming smile he said, "Now, I'll show you my secret fishing places."

LEXIE LEAFED through her mail as she walked from her front gate up the path to her door. It was the third day of an unseasonable heat wave and her steps were slow. Cicadas buzzed in the gardenia bushes lining the path.

Bills, flyers, a letter from her local MP addressed to Householder. A square purple envelope with an American stamp promised to be a late birthday card from her cousin living in California.

A business-size envelope with the Australian Taxation Office logo made her stop where she was in the blazing sun, her heart palpitating in dread... and anticipation. Here it was, at last. She entered the relative cool of the house, kicked off her flip-flops and went into the living room. On the couch, Yang raised his head, blinking sleepily, and stretched out a paw.

Sitting next to him, Lexie left the rest of the mail in her lap while she turned the tax office envelope over. No handwritten return address, nothing to suggest Rafe had sent the letter. She bit her lip, wondering if he'd enclosed a personal note.

She pressed a hand to her flat stomach. A baby.

She hadn't had time to fully process the wonder of it. She didn't deserve another baby. And yet a child was growing inside her. Despite what had happened twenty-one years ago, despite her financial problems and her lack of a partner, despite the fact that she could barely look after herself let alone a child...

She was glad.

But she *did* have financial problems. Serious problems. How could she paint and take care of a child? Sally, in the first months after Chloe was born, had had trouble just finding a few minutes to shower and wash her hair. How would Lexie find the time and concentration necessary to paint? Hetty might help out but she had her own life. Lexie had argued with her father that Hetty deserved time to pursue her interest in yoga and meditation. It wouldn't be fair then for her to foist babysitting on her mother.

If she went back to teaching she could afford childcare. But she'd have to say goodbye to her dream of being a painter. And what good was having a child if she never saw him? Or her?

Other women coped with these issues. She would, too.

She still had to tell Rafe. The thought filled her with dread. He was going to run a mile—from a woman twelve years older than himself, from a baby he didn't want.

Lexie didn't have to tell him right away. Let herself get used to the idea first, figure out how she was going to handle it.

She glanced at the tax office envelope again. It was going to be bad news. She didn't want to read it before she'd finished painting for the day.

Tossing the letter onto the side table along with the flyers, she opened the purple envelope and pulled out a cartoon birthday card. It showed a woman who was mutton dressed as lamb blowing out about a hundred candles.

Lexie burst into tears.

So much for staying positive until she finished

painting. She might as well get all the bad stuff over with at once. Choking back sobs, she picked up the letter from the tax office, her hand shaking. Before she could lose her courage, she opened it, heart racing.

She bypassed the covering letter to look for the summary of her income tax return. Rafe had averaged it over five years. Including interest, the amount owing was $21,390.

Her heart sank. It was worse than he'd said it would be. Then she recalled he'd said something about a fine. She turned the page and what she found made her feel ill.

$10,000.

She sank onto the couch, the letter falling from her trembling fingers. Ten thousand dollars in penalties added to the twenty-one thousand in tax added up to…

An impossible amount of money for her to pay.

Her mind scrabbled for solutions. Her family would help her. But no, they couldn't. Jack had just started a business manufacturing his GPS for small aircraft. Renita had taken out a second mortgage on her house to help Brett refurbish his fitness center. Her mother and father were on a fixed income. She couldn't ask them to advance her a huge sum which she had no guarantee of being able to pay back.

She would have to sell her house. But that would

mean leaving her studio. How would she paint? How would she raise her baby?

Rafe would pay child support. He had to by law. Lexie had only known him a week. She had no idea how he'd react in this situation. He hadn't asked to be a father. But then, she hadn't asked to be a mother.

But all that was beside the point. Child support wouldn't kick in until the baby was born. And Rafe would be helping pay for the baby's needs, not hers.

Lexie wrapped her arms around her waist. She couldn't breathe. How could the fine be so much?

Then she noticed a small piece of notepaper on the couch that must've fallen out. Rafe's strong slanting handwriting jumped up at her.

Lexie, The government is cracking down in this election year, making examples of tax evaders. I was given no choice but to issue the maximum fine. Sorry. Rafe.

Sorry? He was sorry? How did he think *she* felt?

Lexie jumped to her feet. How did he think she was going to come up with thirty-one thousand dollars?

She spun back to the couch and snatched up the letter, looking for the letterhead and the phone number. She would call him. Surely there was some citizen's right of appeal.

She reached for her phone but halfway through punching the number in, she stopped. It was too easy to put someone off over the phone. She'd have better luck going to his office to speak to him in person.

Yes, she would see him in person. Lexie dropped her head in her hands. And after they worked out how she was going to pay her fine, she would tell him about the baby.

CHAPTER NINE

RAFE STEPPED OFF the elevator, swinging a deli bag with his cheeseburger inside, and whistling a tune. Thank God it was Friday. Tomorrow he would head to Mordialloc and take possession of his boat. He'd been carrying the photo of it in his pocket all week, showing it to everyone.

"Hey, Pat. How's it going?" Rafe breezed past the trim, forty-something brunette at reception.

"Larry wants to see you in his office," Pat said. Her next words stopped Rafe in his tracks. "And you're to bring Lexie Thatcher's file."

Oh, hell. Two weeks had passed since he'd filed her return. The letter had gone out a couple of days ago. Rafe had thought he was home free.

"Sure. Thanks, Pat." He made his way more slowly to his desk and riffled in his filing cabinet for Lexie's folder.

Chris glanced up as Rafe trudged by. "What's up?"

Rafe shrugged, avoiding Chris's gaze. Clutching the folder tight under his arm, he wove through the maze of cubicles and around the corner to Larry's office.

The door was ajar. He knocked and pushed it open. "Larry?"

His heart kicked up at the sight of Lexie's slender figure in a cotton dress and her tanned bare legs. Her hair was piled loosely on top of her head, with long curls falling around her face.

Her gaze lasered in on him. "There you are."

"Ms. Thatcher just arrived. We're about to discuss the tax assessment you did for her," Larry said to Rafe. "Have a seat."

Damn and triple damn. Rafe took the chair next to Lexie. He met her gaze, trying to decipher the odd light in her eyes.

Larry's phone rang. As he answered it, Rafe leaned toward her and spoke in a low voice. "What have you said? Don't let on there was anything between us. Strictly business."

Her crystal-clear eyes turned opaque. "We need to talk about that. But it's not what I'm here to discuss right now."

Rafe checked his pocket for the roll of antacid tablets. Quietly, he took one out and popped it in his mouth.

Larry hung up the phone. "Now, Ms. Thatcher. What can we do for you?"

Lexie pulled the envelope with her income tax summary from a big tan leather handbag. "There's been a mistake. The amount I have to pay is too much."

"Rafe is one of our best auditors," Larry said, glancing over it. "I double-checked your file personally. I didn't detect any mistakes in the calculations."

"It's not the tax return I'm worried about." Lexie waved it away with paint-stained fingers. "It's the massive penalties I object to. Yes, I should have declared my income but I wasn't trying to deliberately defraud the tax office. I simply can't afford that much."

"There are options for paying by installments. Your return should have included information about how to do that."

"It did," Rafe said. "In the covering letter. I suggested she call me to talk about it." He turned to Lexie. "Why didn't you phone or email?"

"I want to appeal," Lexie insisted. "I looked this up on your website." She looked back at Rafe accusingly. "You gave me the maximum penalties. After everything we—" She broke off, biting her lip.

A charged silence filled the office. Rafe's palms grew damp.

Frowning, Larry glanced from Rafe to Lexie. He leaned forward. "Go on. what were you about to say? After everything you and Rafe…what?"

Lexie tightened her hands on the straps of her handbag. "I want to talk to Rafe privately."

"Privately?" Larry repeated, making the word sound sordid.

Rafe jumped to his feet. "We don't need to bother you with this, Larry—"

"Sit down," Larry ordered. "We're not done yet."

Rafe wiped a hand across his forehead and sank back into his chair.

"I understand that Rafe spent a week at your house preparing your tax return," Larry said to Lexie.

"I was booked into a bed and breakfast," Rafe interjected. "I worked on her assessment there, too. Part of the time."

"Y-yes," Lexie said, answering Larry's question. She glanced uncertainly at Rafe.

"Rafe has been on probation for getting too in-volved in auditees," Larry said. "So I'm concerned that…irregularities might have occurred." He picked up a pen and twirled it in his fingers. "During the audit, did your relationship with Rafe take on a… personal nature, Ms. Thatcher?"

Lexie's chin came up. "That's none of your business."

"Rafe is working for the government of Australia. It *is* the business of the tax office what goes on during audits." Larry studied his pen, giving that time to sink in. Then he glanced up and repeated his question. "Was your relationship with Rafe personal?"

Lexie went still. "Do I need a lawyer?"

"Just answer the question, please."

Rafe got to his feet again, his stomach full of needles. "Quit harassing her. She didn't do anything wrong."

"Let Ms. Thatcher speak—"

"Why would you even imagine there was something going on between us? She's a whole lot older than me, for one thing." He was being belligerent but he was rattled. "And she's an artist which is *so* not my type. You know me, Larry. Beer and fishing."

"Yes, it was personal," Lexie said quietly. She rose, her face deathly pale. "I'm pregnant with his child."

Rafe reeled, stumbling into the credenza, toppling a potted cactus and spilling dirt. "You…what?"

"You heard me. There's a café on the ground floor. Meet me there in five minutes." She swung back to Larry, whose jaw had fallen open. "My baby is *not* the business of the tax office."

She grabbed her leather handbag and swept out of the office.

BABY? PREGNANT? Had he heard correctly? Rafe stared at the empty space where Lexie had been a few seconds before. Then he lurched out of the office after her, ignoring Larry, who was firing questions as fast as he could spit them out.

Rafe tore around the corner and through the door to reception just in time to see the elevator doors close. He stabbed at the button, backed up, hands on hips. Lexie's elevator was almost at ground level. The light for the second elevator was flashing five floors above.

"What's going on?" Pat asked, ignoring her incoming call. "Who was that woman?"

"An auditee." Giving up on the elevator, he pushed through the fire exit and ran down ten flights of stairs. Bursting through at the ground floor, he skidded to a halt.

Through the glass wall of the café he could see her with her back to him, her slender fingers tightly clasped on the round table. He crossed the lobby and went inside, taking a seat in the booth opposite her.

He'd told himself he wasn't going to touch her but he found himself placing his hands over hers. "What do you mean, you're pregnant? You can't drop a bombshell like that then just walk out."

She withdrew her hands, her expression cool. "I didn't want to talk about it with your boss. He came through reception as I was giving my name to the woman at the desk and he invited me to wait in his office."

"Checking up on me," Rafe muttered.

"I didn't mean to tell you like that," Lexie said. "It just…came out."

"It was a helluva way to find out I'm going to be a—" He couldn't even say it. "You shouldn't have come here. You should have called so we could talk about this privately."

The waiter brought Lexie a latte. Rafe ordered a double espresso. His stomach felt like hell and he wished he'd had a chance to eat his lunch. But he badly needed a coffee.

"Well, here we are," Lexie said. "Let's talk."

"When did you find out? How far along are you?"

"I found out a few days ago." Lexie sipped her coffee. "You're the numbers man. You do the math."

He didn't need a calculator. He'd left Summerside four weeks and three days ago. This wasn't happening. He must be dreaming, although it was more of a nightmare. The waiter brought his espresso and he downed it in one gulp, wincing as the bitter liquid hit his empty stomach.

"How did this happen?" he demanded. "You said—" He stopped, realizing he was practically shouting, and lowered his voice. "You said you had an IUD."

She held herself erect but the strain showed in her face. "It must have slipped out. I didn't notice."

"How can you not notice something like that?" Not that he knew anything about IUDs. She was the only woman he'd been with that had one. Or at least, thought she did.

Or *said* she did.

He stared at her, a suspicion chilling him. "You did this on purpose."

"How could you say such a thing?" Pale before, now she went white. "I would never do that!"

"You wanted a kid. It was obvious to anyone with eyes in their head." He clenched his fists beneath the table. *"I want to go to bed with you, Rafe."*

"I didn't hear you say no." Spots of color now stained her cheeks. "You—" Lexie clamped her mouth shut as a couple passed by on their way to another table. Then she spit out, "You wanted me, too."

God help him, he still wanted her. But he was damned if he'd be that stupid again. Idiot. He *never* had sex without condoms, not even when a woman told him she was on the pill. No...IUD. Now look where he was.

"Are you going to keep it?" he asked.

Her head jerked back as if he'd slapped her. *"It,* Rafe? He or she is a little person, a human being. Yes, I'm going to keep the baby."

"I'm not ready to get married." His voice was tight, every muscle in his body tense.

"Nobody asked you to marry me," Lexie pointed out icily. "I don't want a *boy* for a husband. And since I'm way too old for you—"

Rafe flinched. "I said that upstairs for Larry's benefit."

"Sure." Disbelief and disappointment were etched on her face.

"I'm not ready to be a father, either. If I ever will

be. And that's a big if. I'm trying to get established with this fishing charter business."

"You're all talk," she said, waving a hand. "You're never going to buy a boat."

"I already did." He slid his wallet from his back pocket and removed a bent photo. "I'm going to call it *Someday*."

Blinking, she gazed at the picture, struggling to process the information. Her cheeks paled. "So you'll be quitting your job."

"Hell, no. I can't afford to, not yet." He tucked the photo back in his wallet. Larry would probably fire him anyway. "A baby couldn't come at a worse time for me."

She stood and gathered up her purse. "I don't want anything from you. Not money, not time, nothing. You're clearly too immature to be a father. I only told you because it seemed like the right thing to do. Some men would want to know. I guess you're not one of them."

She brushed past him. His head in his hands, he let her go. He heard the café door open and close.

A boy for a husband? He didn't feel like a boy. He felt as if he'd aged a hundred years.

LEXIE STUMBLED down the street to the off-road parking lot where she'd left her car. Her legs didn't seem to be moving properly. Her face felt stiff with the effort not to cry. Rafe—what an absolute jerk.

Only now did she realize that some tiny part of her had been hoping that he might actually want the baby. What a fool she'd been!

If he could think she'd gotten pregnant on purpose then quite likely he'd also thought she would try to trap him into marriage.

She fumbled for her keys and unlocked her door. When she was safely inside she put her head down on the steering wheel and let the tears flow.

Bastard. She hated him. How dare he? *How dare he?*

Someone knocked on her window. She tried to stop crying. He'd come after her. He was sorry. He—
She raised her head.

A woman of about sixty, well dressed with a blond pageboy and heavy gold earrings, peered in at her.

Lexie rolled down the window.

The woman handed her a tissue, gold bracelets clinking. "Are you all right, honey?" she said in a raspy voice. "I watched you all the way down the block."

Wiping her wet eyes with the tissue, Lexie shook her head. "Men are pigs."

The woman nodded. "You got that right. You probably shouldn't drive when you're that upset."

Lexie let out a deep, shuddering sigh. "I'll sit here and listen to the radio for a while. Thanks."

The woman walked away, glancing back over her shoulder. Lexie mustered a smile and waved.

She checked herself in the mirror and saw a bleary, haggard face. No wonder the woman had been worried.

She wiped away the rest of her tears. To hell with Rafe. She didn't need him. She could do this on her own.

Instead of turning on the radio she closed her eyes and leaned back against the headrest.

She was a crystal lying on the sandy bottom of a quiet pond. Calm and—

Rafe's face appeared before her, destroying her peace. His sexy body, handsome face with the black stubble and bedroom eyes. Bedroom. That's where all the trouble had started.

It wasn't all trouble. She wanted this baby. Lexie squirmed, agitated by the conflicting emotions.

Stop thinking! Just breathe.

She was as smooth and round as a washed pebble but perfectly clear. Crystal clear.

He'd wanted her to terminate the pregnancy. As if that would solve all their problems. He didn't have any idea.

She dug her phone out of her purse and checked for messages. With a few minutes to process, he might—

None. Damn. She snapped the phone shut and tossed it on the passenger seat.

Closing her eyes again, she made an effort to slow her breathing. *Peace...calm...light—*

Tears seeped from beneath her closed lids.

It was no good trying to meditate in a parking lot on a busy street when she was distressed. She started the car and set off for Summerside, glad of the distraction of dealing with traffic to take her mind off Rafe, her taxes, the baby.

Gradually an icy calm settled over her. She would do what she had to do to survive.

When she got home she went around her studio and house and rounded up every seascape painting she'd completed. There were five—two of Morningston Pier and the fishing boats, one of Summerside village, one of the creek among the trees behind her house with the cool green filtered light.

The fifth was the full moon rising above Summerside Beach while the sky was aglow with sunset. When she pulled that one out she had to concentrate so hard not to cry that she got a headache.

Don't think about him.

She cleared the long trestle table and brought out colored sheets of mat board, the mat cutter, a ruler and a pencil. She spent the rest of the day framing the paintings.

Sienna's portrait sat propped on its easel to one side, a reminder of what she wanted to be doing. But she didn't have the luxury anymore of doing only what she wanted. Still it was a dilemma—the guaranteed but small income from the commercial paintings, or the uncertain but potentially large cash prize of the Archibald.

Somehow, she had to do both. As she worked she calculated in her head how much she could hope to earn from the sale of these paintings. She would put it toward the usual food, mortgage and utility bills plus save a portion for the baby and a portion for her tax bill. She didn't know what she'd do if her earnings didn't cover everything. Paint faster?

A painting under each arm, she crossed the lawn and rounded the side of the house into the carport. She'd just opened the trunk of her car when the phone rang. She raced inside to answer it.

"Hello?"

"Hey, Lexie," Jack said. "How's everything?"

"You're back! Welcome home. I'm fine," she added. She wasn't ready to tell anyone else about her pregnancy.

"Can you come for dinner tonight? A kind of post-wedding, post-honeymoon celebration. Just the family."

She was dead tired but this was special if Jack was issuing a formal invitation. "Sure, I can make it. Are Mum and Dad both coming?"

"Yes." Jack said firmly. "Sienna and I want tonight to be an opportunity for the two of them to be together without any outside influences, if you catch my drift."

"That's a great idea." She glanced at the wall

clock. "Jack, I've got to run to the gallery before it closes. I'll see you tonight."

The Manyung Gallery held major shows of one or two prominent artists at a time. They usually ran for six weeks. They also carried paintings and sculptures from local artists—including Lexie—on an ongoing basis. Normally Samuel, the owner, didn't have space for more than three or four.

Tall and spare with thinning blond hair, Samuel was dressed in a pale pink shirt and tan pants. He was standing before a painting, discussing it with a potential customer, an older woman in a dark blue dress. Lexie carried two of her paintings inside, nodding to him.

Seeing her carrying in paintings, he frowned before turning back to his customer. When she went back out to the car and came back with three more, he handed the woman to his young blonde assistant, Tanya.

"Lexie, love," Samuel said, hurrying over. "I can't take any more of your paintings till the others sell."

She blinked. "What do you mean?"

"Your wall is still full. Come and see for yourself."

Fear seized her. She'd been so busy with Rafe and her portrait she hadn't paused to wonder why she hadn't heard about any sales.

Samuel led her to the alcove where her paintings

were always hung. Three paintings. Not one bore a little orange Sold sticker.

"I did as you asked and raised the price. Nothing's moved." He crossed his arms, eyebrows lifted, letting her draw her own conclusions.

Lexie's heart sank. This was a huge setback. She'd been counting on these sales to pay this month's bills. Summer and early autumn were her most profitable months, when tourists came to holiday on the peninsula. If she couldn't sell now...

This is what she got for being greedy. No, not greedy. She'd been showing off in front of Rafe, not wanting him to think she didn't have a business bone in her body.

She smiled weakly, feeling sick inside. "I guess I owe you a bottle of pinot noir."

"What do you want to do?" Samuel said. "Shall we lower the price a tad?"

Lexie nodded heavily. "Drop them to where they'll sell."

Then she had to watch while he took out a pen and slashed the price.

She gestured to her new paintings. "Can you store these until there's space to hang them?"

"Carry them into the back room. I'll get the book to record what we've got." Samuel started to move toward the reception desk then paused. "Are you okay? You look tired."

Lexie forced a smile, knowing it didn't reach her

eyes. "I'm wonderful. Couldn't be better. Excuse me, I'll just use your washroom before I go."

"You take care." Samuel gave her a hug and walked away.

Lexie went into the public restroom and found a cubicle. She'd forgotten how often she'd had to pee when she was last pregnant; every hour it seemed. She pulled down her underwear and her breath caught in her throat.

Bright red blood stained her white panties.

CHAPTER TEN

SWAYING SLIGHTLY on his stool, Rafe held up a finger
to the bartender Rick…or Rob—a forty-something
man with a shaved head whose neutral expression
never seemed to vary. "'Nother round."

By the time he'd gotten back to the office after
talking to Lexie, Larry had gone off to a meeting that
Pat told him would likely last most of the afternoon.
Rafe had headed straight to the bar. He'd been drinking shots of tequila with a beer chaser ever since.
Chris had come out with him for a couple of hours
before heading off to meet Laura.

Rafe downed another tequila. After Chris left he'd
wandered the street going from pub to pub and ended
up downstairs in Jackson's. The Friday after-work
crowd swirled around him at the long polished bar,
eating tapas and drinking cocktails.

Every so often the thought reared up and smacked
him in the head. He was going to be a father.

"I don' wanna be a father," he said to the bartender, "I have plans. I'm too young to settle down.
Too frickin' young. Aren't I, Rick?"

"My name is Raoul." He had an accent—Spanish?

His hands moved like a magician's as he poured vodka and three or four other ingredients into a cocktail shaker.

"Raoouul?" It sounded like a wolf howling. That's what Rafe felt like doing, howling.

"You're drunk." The woman sitting next to him in a business suit took the frothy pink vodka Raoul handed her and eyed Rafe in disgust. "I pity the woman."

"Who asked you?" Rafe muttered, and reached for his beer. He glanced up at Raoul. "I asked for another tequila."

"Sorry, mate," the bartender said, polishing a glass. "I have to cut you off. I'll call you a cab."

"Never mind. I'll take the train." Rafe placed a twenty on the bar and stumbled outside.

The pub was located on the busiest corner in Melbourne. Flinders Street train station, golden domed and ornately Victorian, stood across six lanes of rush hour traffic. Rafe stepped off the curb. Horns blared. Someone grabbed the back of his shirt and hauled him to the sidewalk.

"Moron," said the man, and let him go so abruptly Rafe fell to his knees on the pavement.

"He's a drunk," his wife said, full of revulsion.

"No, I'm a tax accountant," Rafe said, holding up a finger. "And a fisherman. You wanna see a picture of my boat?"

The light changed. Pedestrians streamed around

him and across the street. Rafe was left on the other side, marooned on his knees, gazing at the crumpled photo of his boat.

LEXIE USUALLY LOVED dinner parties at Jack's house. Jack and *Sienna's* house, she amended. She had to get used to the changes in her family. Sienna had put her house on the market and moved into Jack's home after they'd returned from their honeymoon in Bali. Sienna's house was in a nicer location but it was smaller and Jack's workshop was right next door to his place.

Jack's dinner parties were full of laughter and conversation and good food. Usually Lexie couldn't wait to get right in the thick of it. Not tonight, though. She never told her family *everything* that went on in her life.

But this was a baby.

She should let them know. She wasn't sure why she hadn't. Probably she was a little embarrassed to have been careless enough to get pregnant. At her age.

The spotting on her panties worried her. Why hadn't she called Natalie? Her excuse was that she was too busy, but that was foolish. Was she in denial, afraid to admit that something was wrong?

She paused at the entrance to the open plan kitchen and dining room, taking in the scene. Jack and Renita were at the stove, teasing each other as Jack put finishing touches on his dish—lamb with garlic and rosemary, judging by the aroma.

Hetty was chatting to Oliver and Tegan while the two teenagers set the table. Steve and Brett stood at the counter, beer in hand, no doubt discussing the coming football season. Steve was looking fitter as his regular workouts at the gym had started to pay off.

Sienna, wearing a batik skirt she must have bought in Bali and a black, scoop-necked top, greeted Lexie with a hug. Lexie clung to the other woman for a moment. "Sorry I didn't bring anything. I…I just didn't have time. Or, frankly, the energy."

"Don't you even think about that." Sienna eased back, frowning, to search Lexie's face. "You look tired. Have you lost weight?"

"Maybe a pound or two," Lexie said. It wasn't surprising she was run-down. She worked from morning till night, alternately painting Sienna's portrait when the light was the best and the smaller seascapes for Samuel's gallery. "Are fumes from the oil paints and the turpentine bad for…me?"

Jack was approaching as she spoke. "You've never worried about that before," he commented before Sienna could reply. He held up two bottles of wine for Lexie to choose. "Red or white?"

"Neither," Lexie said. "I'll just have mineral water."

"Are you sick?" Renita asked, pausing on her

way from the kitchen to the table with a basket of fresh rolls. "I've never heard you turn down wine before."

"I'm just tired." Lexie was more than tired—she was struggling not to collapse on the spot. "And I have to be up early tomorrow to paint."

"Are you going to get the portrait done in time?" Renita asked.

"I hope so," Lexie said. "I've only got a couple more weeks before it has to be transported to Sydney."

"You'll get there," Renita assured her, and continued on to the table. Jack went with her, carrying the wine.

"Is there any particular reason you asked about the paints and solvents?" Sienna regarded her closely.

"I…I've been spending a lot of time in the studio lately."

"Keep the room well ventilated. You should limit your exposure as much as possible." Sienna paused. "Is there anything else?"

"Um. Actually…" Lexie glanced around to make sure no one was listening. "What does it mean when there's spotting during pregnancy? Is it a sign of a miscarriage?"

Sienna's gray-green eyes seemed to see straight into Lexie. But she merely replied, "Not necessarily. Spotting in early pregnancy is the mother's blood, not the baby's. It can be because the placenta isn't firmly attached to the uterus wall." She hesitated, and then lowered her voice. "Are you—?"

"Here you are!" Renita presented Lexie with a glass of mineral water. She held out a plate of tiny pancakes topped with smoked salmon. "Dad made these, would you believe it? Try one. They're great."

"Thanks." Lexie took an appetizer. She glanced at Sienna. "Talk later?"

"Sure. For now, why don't you sit down." Sienna put her arm around Lexie's waist and walked her to the table while Renita circulated with the hors d'oeuvres.

Lexie sank gratefully into a chair and sipped her mineral water. Sienna's comments made her feel a little better. The spotting was probably nothing to worry about.

"Hey, Lexie," Tegan said as she came around laying plates while Oliver followed with cutlery. "Your hair looks pretty."

"Thanks." She touched her hastily pinned up hair. At least someone wasn't commenting on how awful she looked. "I like your top," she said of the black-and-purple ripped shirt. "Very retro."

"Dad hates it," Tegan confided.

"Men. What do they know?" Lexie turned to greet Oliver. "Hey, buddy, could you come over and cut my lawn sometime? It's started to grow again. I'll pay you."

"Is next week okay?" Oliver said, dropping knives and forks haphazardly.

"Perfect." It was another expense but her time was more profitably spent painting. Hetty sank into the chair next to her. "How's it going?" she asked her mum in a low voice laced with a smile. "Is the Orgasmitron Five Hundred working its magic?"

"Shh, not so loud," Hetty said. "You don't want the kids to think the oldies are having sex."

"Well, are you?" Lexie took an olive from the dish on the table and popped it in her mouth. Instantly she spit it out, frowning at it. She loved olives but this one tasted wrong somehow.

Ignoring that, Hetty glanced over at Steve. "We had a big fight after Sienna and Jack's wedding reception. He thinks I overreacted to Susan Dwyer's presence. We're living in a state of armed truce. It's like Europe after World War II. I swear, I don't know what else I can do."

"Dinner's up," Jack called, carrying a platter of slow-roasted lamb with roasted vegetables to the table.

When everyone had sat down, Jack raised his wineglass. "To family."

"Hear, hear," Lexie murmured, and sipped her mineral water. She'd always taken her close-knit family for granted, but she was going to need her parents and siblings more than ever in the coming months. She noticed Steve had chosen a chair as far from Hetty as possible and frowned. Damn it, she needed them to be together.

The next few minutes were taken up with passing food down the table, topping up drinks and running back to the kitchen for forgotten items. Then everyone was eating. Talk had reduced to comments about the delicious food.

"So, Mum, Dad," Jack began conversationally. "When are you two going to take that trip around Australia you've been talking about for years?"

Silence. Not even the clink of forks on plates as everyone looked at Hetty and Steve. *They* looked everywhere but at each other.

Steve cleared his throat. "I've got speeches at the club lined up over the next few months. I'm working my way through the manual."

"And I have commitments with my yoga group," Hetty said.

Lexie exchanged glances with Jack and Renita. No one said anything.

Then Hetty put her knife and fork down. "Come now, Steve. We're not fooling anyone. We'd be at each other's throats if we were cooped up together on a long road trip."

"You're not interested in traveling anyway," Steve complained. "You're not interested in anything I am."

"I could say the same about you," Hetty retorted.

"Never mind," Sienna interjected. "We don't need

to talk about this while we're eating dinner. It'll spoil our digestion. Right, Jack?" she added pointedly, with a warning glance.

"It's good they're talking," Jack argued. "How are they going to settle their differences otherwise?"

"Do they need to do it in front of the children?" Sienna asked, nodding to Oliver and Tegan. "It'll lead to an argument."

"I'm not a child," Tegan piped up.

"I don't want them to fight in front of *me,*" Renita said. "They need to work it out themselves."

Then everyone but Lexie was speaking at once, the volume escalating as individuals struggled to be heard. Lexie pressed her fingers to her aching temple.

"Quiet, please!" Picking up a spoon, she tapped on her water glass till the cacophony died down. "I have an idea."

All heads turned to her. "Mum, join Toastmasters and go to the meetings. Dad, learn to meditate—"

"Meditate? No way," Steve protested automatically.

"Why not?" Lexie demanded. "You can do yoga, too. You're into fitness now and yoga's excellent for strength and flexibility. Isn't it, Brett?"

Brett, who was still paying off a loan from Renita to buy the gym, nodded. "I'm putting it on the program."

"There you go." Lexie swayed, suddenly dizzy in her seat. But she was determined to get an agreement out of her parents. "So, you two. We've all heard enough complaining about the other person. Will you do something to fix your marriage? Before long there will be grandchildren on the way. Wouldn't it be nice to share that joy together?"

"Grandchildren?" Hetty said, looking from Renita to Sienna. "Did I miss something?"

Eyes wide, Renita glanced at Sienna, who shook her head.

Too late, Lexie realized she'd put her foot in her mouth. She'd planned to tell her family the news when she'd gotten through the first trimester and was more financially stable. "I mean, Sienna and Renita will *probably* be starting new families in the foreseeable future." Beads of perspiration formed on her forehead and temples. She blinked and glanced desperately at Sienna. "Right?"

"Yes," Sienna said, a worried frown on her face.

"Mum, if you're going to teach yoga, public speaking skills would come in handy. And Dad, meditation is a stress reliever, good for general health. And for both of you, this would be a way of spending time together, understanding each other…."

Spots appeared before her eyes. "Ooh." The room went blurry. Then black.

When Lexie came to she was lying under a blanket on Jack's brown leather couch in the living room. Sienna was sitting on the coffee table, taking her pulse. The rest of the family crowded them anxiously.

Lexie struggled to sit up. Her hair was damp from perspiration and her throat was dry but the dizziness had passed. "I'm fine."

Sienna adjusted the cushions and held a cup to her lips. "Drink this."

Lexie took a sip and cool water soothed her throat. She met Sienna's gaze. "Thanks."

"Is she sick?" Hetty asked, taking Lexie's hand. "Should she go to Emergency?"

"She's overworked, that's all," Sienna replied. "But you should probably see your doctor, Lexie. Soon," she added meaningfully.

"I'll bring you your plate," Brett said. "We could all move in here, eat off our laps."

"I'm not very hungry…." Lexie began.

Sienna brushed her hair back. "You should eat."

"Don't push food on her if she's not hungry," Renita said, leaning on the back of the couch. As someone who'd lost weight and continued to struggle to stay fit, she was sensitized to the issue. "All the weight loss experts say that's how people gain, by eating when they don't need to."

Steve, the type 2 diabetic, stood at Lexie's feet. "You know how she forgets to eat when she's painting. Her blood sugar's probably low."

"Enough!" Lexie flung her hands up. Everyone stared expectantly at her. "Thank you for your concern but... Oh, God, I might as well tell you. Yes, I'm overworked but I'm not sick." She paused a beat. "I'm pregnant."

There was a shocked silence, then pandemonium broke out. Questions, congratulations, expressions of concern for her health, her ability to provide for herself and her child. Lexie's struggle to make ends meet was no secret.

"Hold on," Steve said in a loud voice. "We're forgetting the most important thing. Who's the father?"

Lexie groaned inwardly, knowing what was coming. "Rafe."

Steve looked blank. "Rafe who?"

"The tax accountant who was auditing her," Hetty said, beaming. "He's lovely."

"I don't think I met him," Jack said.

"He was only here a week," Sienna explained.

"That was some audit, Lexie," Renita said, smiling.

"A week?" Steve said, incredulous. "You're pregnant by a guy you knew for a week?"

Her father's negative reaction set the rest of them off again, talking over, across and around her. Lexie shut her eyes. She loved her family to bits but sometimes she wished they would all just go away.

Then she opened her eyes again and tried to catch Steve's attention. "Excuse me, Dad." He was asking Sienna about pregnancy and blood sugar. "Dad!"

"What is it, sweetheart?"

She glanced at Hetty to include her. "Will you two go together to Toastmasters and yoga?"

Steve and Hetty glanced at Lexie, then at each other, warily. Neither seemed willing to speak first.

"Do it for your grandchild," Renita admonished quietly.

At the thought of a grandbaby Hetty brightened. Then she glanced at Steve and stopped smiling.

Lexie started to lose hope. "Please, Mum."

Hetty wavered another long moment. "Yes, all right."

All eyes turned to Steve. Finally, he said gruffly, "If I can stand up and give a speech I guess it'd be a snap to meditate. Heck, they just sit around and say nothing. And I'll do yoga as long as I don't have to wear a leotard."

"Thank you," Lexie said, relieved they were going to try.

And that they'd stopped talking about Rafe.

RAFE STRUGGLED against the return to consciousness. His eyes were glued shut. He had the mother of all headaches and a thirst bigger than the outback. He could hear the rumble of train wheels, feel the vibration through his seat. He was leaning against the wall, a strip of cool metal beneath his left cheek. The frame around a window.

He rubbed his eyes, blinked a few times. It took a moment to focus. When he did, he sat up straight.

It was broad daylight.

Wheat fields stretched to the horizon, broken by the ragged and meandering row of river red gums that told of a dried-up creek bed running roughly parallel to the tracks.

Holy hell. This sure wasn't Sassafras.

He glanced at his watch. Eleven o'clock.

"Excuse me," he said to a trio of teenage boys sitting in facing seats across the aisle. Dressed in jeans and plaid shirts, they held felt hats in their laps. Ten years ago, before he'd left for the city, he'd looked very much as they did. "Where are we?"

"Western District," a boy with gelled blond hair said. "Next town is Horsham."

The other two teens sniggered. One said, "Don't you know where you're going?"

Rafe rubbed a hand through his hair. It felt dirty and oily. Looking down, he saw that his shirt was creased and stained and there was a rip in his pants over the right knee. "Sure I do," he said slowly. "I'm going to see my folks."

He just didn't know why. Or what he was going to tell them when he got there.

Twenty minutes later, Rafe stepped onto the platform, squinting in the bright sunlight unbroken by cloud or trees. With a whistle blow, the train chugged off for Adelaide. He followed the other disembarking passengers into the station and stopped to look at the schedule. The train back to Melbourne wasn't coming through until tomorrow.

Stepping outside into the shade of the broad eaves, he pulled out his cell phone and dialed his mother's cell phone. "Mum?" he said when she picked up.

"Rafe!" she said. "Where are you?"

"At the train station. Any chance you could come and get me?"

"I'm at work. Is something wrong?"

"Why should there be something wrong?"

"Because we don't hear from you from one month to the next and then you turn up out of the blue…" She trailed off but he could hear her exasperation. "You're not in trouble, are you?"

"There've been… I could take a taxi." He glanced toward the empty taxi stand. If a guy could even find a cab in this one-horse burg.

"No, no. I'll be there in about fifteen minutes."

"Thanks." Rafe hung up and walked back into the station. He bought a bottle of water out of the vending machine and downed it in one long chug. At least when he got to the house he could get some painkillers for this hangover.

His mother came for him in a dusty white Ford that backfired as she came to a halt out front of the station. She was wearing her uniform from the pharmacy—navy pants and a red-and-navy flowered top. She was dark, like him, with her thick black hair tamed into a ponytail.

Rafe climbed in and gave her a peck on the cheek. "Car could use a tune-up."

Ellen Ellersley stared at him. "What happened to you? Your clothes are filthy and torn. You've got dirt on your cheek. Your hair makes you look like a wild man."

"Is that all?" Rafe asked, grinning. "That's not so bad."

"You stink to high heaven." She shook her head but her voice softened as she asked again, "What happened?"

Rafe looked straight ahead. "I went out for a few drinks after work before I caught the train."

"A few?" Ellen asked drily.

She put the car in gear and drove through the quiet streets of the country town to drop him off at home, a pale green house on a corner lot with a wide paved path to the door and a ramp instead of steps. "I'll be back in a couple of hours."

"Thanks, Mum." He gripped her in an awkward one-arm hug. "I appreciate it."

"Oh, Rafe." She gave him a tired smile. "It's good to see you, even if you do look like something the cat dragged in."

Rafe let himself into the house and toed off his shoes to walk sock foot down the hall to his old room. He found a pair of old jeans and a T-shirt in his dresser and carried them back down the hall to the bathroom. He pushed open the door. And just about jumped out of his skin.

His father was swinging himself off the frame around the toilet with his powerful arms, onto his wheelchair. His pants were still half down around his naked butt.

"Jeez, Dad, you scared the shit out of me." Rafe studied the floor, reluctantly adding, "Do you need help?"

"You know I don't." Darryl Ellersley braced his elbows on the arms of his chair to yank his loose-fitting trousers up to his waist. His coarse sandy hair was flattened on one side as if he'd just gotten out of bed. "What are you doing here?"

"I came on a whim." He's aged, Rafe thought with a pang of regret. He really should see his parents more often. Stepping aside as his father wheeled out of the bathroom, he said, "I'm going to have a shower, okay?"

"'Course. Smells as if you need one." Darryl spun the chair and gripped Rafe's hand. "You might want to ask if your boss could spring for a clothing allowance, too…. Good to see you, son."

Rafe showered and changed into clean clothes. He walked to the kitchen, barefoot, hair still dripping.

His father had pulled his chair up to the table, a steaming mug in front of him. "Kettle's boiled. Help yourself to something to eat."

"You want anything?"

"Nah, I'm fine." Darryl pulled the paper over and turned to the crossword.

Rafe spooned instant coffee into a mug and poured in the water. He got milk out of the fridge then went back for eggs and ham. Setting the frying pan on the stove, he asked, "How's the clock repair business?"

"I'm run off my feet."

"Good one, Dad."

Darryl penciled in a couple of crossword answers. "How's the tax business?"

"Fine."

His father glanced up. "Now tell me the truth."

Rafe cracked an egg into the pan and added a slice of ham. He slotted bread into the toaster. Finally, he admitted, "I'm probably going to get fired over my last audit."

Darryl pointed his pencil at Rafe. "You're too softhearted. People take advantage of you."

"It wasn't like that."

His father waited. That was one thing about the old man being in a wheelchair for so many years. He'd acquired a patience that meant he could outlast anyone.

"We...had an affair."

Darryl snorted and looked back at his crossword. "What's a three-letter word for donkey?"

Rafe flipped his eggs and ham onto a plate. Popping up the toaster before the toast was brown, he slathered it with butter. Sitting, he stared at his plate. "That's not all. She's pregnant."

"That was bloody stupid," Darryl said, scowling. "Didn't I teach you to always use a condom?"

Rafe started eating. "Thought she was safe."

"Are you sure the baby's yours?" Darryl asked. "Some women get knocked up, they just want a ride on the gravy train. I'd get a paternity test before I handed over any support payments, if I was you."

Rafe stopped chewing. A paternity test.

"Nah, Lexie would know if the baby could be someone else's." He forked up another bite of egg and ham.

"Still, it wouldn't hurt to ask."

CHAPTER ELEVEN

"WHAT ARE YOU going to do?" Ellen had come home from work and changed into jeans and a T-shirt. Now she'd tied an apron on and was mixing up meat loaf. His father had gone to his workshop leaving Rafe to tell his mother about Lexie, the baby and the work debacle.

"Babies scare me." Rafe sat at the kitchen table peeling potatoes. "'Give me food, change my diaper, look after me for the next umpteen years.'"

Ellen chuckled as she sprinkled herbs in with the meat. "It's different when they're your own."

"How? In what way is it different?" Rafe demanded. To him all babies looked the same. Behaved the same way. Had the same debilitating effect on their parents. "It seems worse, if anything. Ever since my friends Chris and Laura had Jordon they have no time for anything else anymore."

"You don't want to go out as much when you have children. You love them too much to want to be away from them." Ellen slid the pan of meat loaf into the oven. "Your father was only twenty-one when you were born. I was barely nineteen. He didn't hesitate, not for a second. As soon as I found out I was pregnant he asked me to marry him."

"But you were in love, weren't you?"

Ellen smiled as she wiped her hands. "Yes, we were in love. The only difficult decision we had to make was whether or not Darryl would go to sea while I was pregnant." She fell silent, her mouth drooping. "Well, you know how that turned out."

Rafe dropped a potato into the pot of cold water and reached for another. "There's something I haven't told you or Dad yet. Lexie's thirty-eight."

"Thirty-eight!" Ellen began cutting up the potatoes Rafe had peeled. "What was she thinking, getting mixed up with someone so much younger?"

"We weren't doing a lot of thinking," Rafe said. "Not that her age matters. She doesn't want to marry me."

"Thirty-eight." Ellen placed the cut potatoes back in the pot. "I'm not sure I like this woman."

"Everyone likes Lexie." He was silent a moment. "Did you ever regret getting married and having a baby so young?"

Ellen didn't answer right away. Her knife hit the cutting board in short sharp thunks. With her head bowed he couldn't read her expression.

"Mom?" Rafe said. "Did you have regrets?"

"I wanted to be a nurse." She glanced up with a wistful smile. "I got my wish, only not the way I expected. After the accident your father needed a lot of care."

"You could go back and do your training now."

She glanced at him as if considering it. Then she shook her head. "Nah." Putting down her knife, she gave Rafe a fierce hug. "I never regretted having *you*, not for a second."

Rafe returned the hug, then eased back. "Hey, look at this." He pulled the photo of his boat from his wallet. "Isn't she a beauty? Fifty-foot, twin four-fifty diesel engines. Goes like stink."

Ellen's head came up. "It's yours?"

"I bought her last week. I'll probably be paying for her for the rest of my natural life but yeah, she's mine. I'm going to run a fishing charter. Someday." He smiled. "Name of the boat. *Someday*."

"Oh, Rafe. Congratulations. This is wonderful." Ellen handed him back the photo. "Did you show your father?"

"No." Rafe tucked it away. Slowly, he said, "I guess I didn't want to rub in the fact that I'm going to realize my dream when Dad never got to go after his."

"Honey, your father is proud of you." Ellen blinked, her smile teary. "He'd be pleased that you've achieved this."

Rafe glanced up quickly. "You think so?"

"Absolutely." She carried on chopping potatoes. Thoughtfully, she added, "Sometimes you don't know what you want until it happens. Don't be too quick to write off fatherhood. And forget what I said about not liking Lexie. That was just me being protective of my son. You stand by the mother, do you hear?"

"I'll do the right thing."

If he could only figure out what that was.

MONDAY MORNING, Rafe walked into Larry's office and placed his letter of resignation on top of the file his boss was reading. On the train home from Horsham he'd decided that he could either wait, like a coward, for the ax to come down or fall on his sword.

"What's this?" Larry said before looking up. He frowned when he saw it was Rafe. "Trying to beat me to the punch, I see. Why did you do such a stupid-ass thing, anyway?"

Once-in-a-lifetime sex didn't seem like the kind of answer Larry was looking for so Rafe kept quiet.

Larry picked up Rafe's letter. He read it over, shaking his head. "Damn it, Rafe. You realize I have no choice but to accept this."

Rafe worked his jaw. He'd harbored a faint hope that Larry would tear it up. "Do you want me to stay till you find a replacement or clean out my desk now?"

"We're seriously behind in these assessments…" Larry's face scrunched as he considered the problem. Then he waved a hand. "No, forget it. You blew it. You're out."

Rafe cleared his throat. "Will you give me a reference?"

"Go," Larry said, glaring at him.

"Right." Rafe walked to the door. "Larry? I'm sorry."

Larry didn't look up from his file. Rafe hesitated, and then turned away.

He trudged back to his cubicle past rows of accountants beavering away. Hands in his pockets, shoulders hunched, he tried to come to grips with the fact that he no longer worked at the tax office. Would no longer draw a paycheck.

The shame ate him hollow. He hated leaving this way. Sure, the job was tedious but in tax accounting he was an expert. What did he know about running a fishing charter?

Tina, a petite redhead, popped up to peer over her partition. "Rafe, can you spare a minute? I need some numbers crunched in a hurry."

Any other time, no matter how busy he was, he would have helped out. "Sorry, Tina, no can do."

"Oh," Tina said, surprised. "Are you sure?"

"I'm sure." Rafe left before she could ask any questions. He was in no mood to explain.

He grabbed an empty box from the printer room for his personal things. At least Larry wasn't standing over him—he trusted Rafe enough not to steal the stationery or sabotage computer files.

"What's going on?" Chris stood in the cubicle

doorway as Rafe started dumping his coffee cup and his photos into the box.

Rafe just looked at him. "I'm toast."

"You're fired?" Chris jerked to attention as if preparing to charge Larry's office.

"I beat him to the punch by a millisecond."

"No way. Over Lexie?"

"Don't waste your protest march on me, mate." Rafe moved on to his drawers. "I'm guilty as charged. I lost my independent state of mind."

"But…" Chris's fists balled impotently.

Rafe had told his friend everything last Friday. There was no point in rehashing it; he just wanted to get out of here. He was relieved when Chris's phone rang and he had to answer it.

He continued to pack his personal items. Besides the coffee mug and photos, there was a comb, a roll of antacid tablets, novelty Christmas gifts he'd been given over the years, plus sundry other bits and pieces. The mundane task gave him a moment to regroup. It had been an emotional few days what with Lexie's announcement, telling his parents.

Resigning. Getting fired. Take your pick.

He picked up the Snoopy figurine on the top of his partition wall. Snoopy on his doghouse, fantasizing about shooting down the Red Baron. Turning it over in his hands, he thought of all the times he'd looked at it and longed to chuck the job and go fishing.

Now he was going to do it.

"Here, you go, mate," he said, handing Snoopy to Chris when he finished his phone call. "I pass you the torch."

Clasping the box under one arm, he held out his hand. The reality of his departure was starting to sink in. "I'll keep in touch. You and Laura have to come out on my boat."

Chris gripped his hand and pulled him into a man hug. "I'll bring the champagne to crack over the bow. Don't forget to call me."

"No worries." His smile forced, Rafe walked backward a few steps then spun and strode away.

LEXIE IGNORED her rumbling stomach and concentrated on her brushstrokes. The spotting had stopped after a day, thank God, so, despite Sierra's warnings and her own worries, she hadn't bothered going back to see her doctor. Truly, she simply didn't have time.

But she was so tired she was almost swaying on her feet. She had to get Sienna's skin tone just…right while the light was good. She was minutes away from completing the portrait. She stepped back to survey her work critically, then added more colors to her palette, mixing and applying, layer after layer, racing against the sun's movement across the sky. When it dropped behind the trees lining the creek, her best working hours were finished.

In spite of her fatigue, she felt a quiet excitement

building inside her. Months of effort and long hours, half a dozen different versions, the agony and frustration of being blocked, the exhilaration of incorporating the molecular structure of DNA—it had all culminated in these final moments. It was hard to put down the brush, to make the decision to stop.

But she had to. The deadline had been creeping up and now it was here. The paint wouldn't be completely dry but she couldn't wait any longer. She needed to frame the painting, then crate it and have it shipped to Sydney today.

From the house she could hear the vacuum cleaner going as Hetty cleaned for her. Lexie tried to block the sound. Now that her family knew she was pregnant they all wanted to help. She was grateful, she really was, but having anyone in the house was a distraction. All she wanted to do was finish the portrait and get it to Sydney.

Then she could figure out the rest of her life.

The vacuum cleaner turned off. Lexie's shoulders relaxed. She touched her brush in the white paint and started to put the final, almost microscopic, dabs of highlight on Sienna's cheek that would give her skin a luminous quality.

"Lexie, I'm going to the store now," Hetty said from the doorway. "Have you made a list of groceries?"

Her fingers tightened around the thin wooden brush. "No, Mum," she said without looking around.

"Just get anything that's quick and easy to cook. But healthy." A second later she remembered to say, "Thank you."

"I'll be back shortly," Hetty said, and left.

Alone at last.

She glanced out the window. Only five minutes or so left. If she could just finish…

Someone was standing in the doorway to the studio. She could sense a presence even though no one had spoken. It was probably Renita. She'd said she might drop by this afternoon.

"I'll just be a minute, Renita," Lexie said. "Do you want to go put the kettle on?" In other words, wait in the house.

Concentrating, she finished the last strokes. Finally she put down her brush and arched her back to stretch it, hands on her hips, as she stepped back and critically assessed her painting. It was good.

It was…done.

Oh my God. She was finally finished. Unexpected tears welled in her eyes. She wiped them away, smiling. Finally, it was over. And she was happy with the painting. Happier than with anything else she'd ever painted.

Just one more thing…. She dipped a fine brush in dark red. In the lower right-hand corner she signed her name in flowing script.

A smile on her lips, she turned.

Rafe.

She jerked back, knocking the table holding her palette. Tubes of paint spilled to the floor. She crouched to retrieve them, thankful for the distraction. "W-what are you doing here?"

He was leaning against her doorjamb, arms crossed. "I've come to talk."

Lexie's mouth dried. She drank in his long lean frame in a T-shirt and dark denim, the three-day stubble and thick shock of black hair. And those eyes, deep and dark, studying her.

Then she remembered that the last time she'd seen him she'd cried.

His eyes went to her painting. "I like it," he said, nodding to the easel. "The background was a stroke of genius."

She didn't need his praise, didn't need anything from him. "It's done. That's all I care about. Now I just need to ship it."

He pushed off the door frame, jammed his hands in his back pockets. "Can you spare a few minutes? We need to talk," he repeated. "About the baby."

Lexie's gaze dropped to his sock feet. Her defenses nearly crumbled. He didn't want to be a father but he'd remembered to take off his shoes in her house. "Just let me clean up."

She slotted her used brushes into the jar of turpentine and wiped her stained fingers with a turps-soaked rag. Then she pulled off her smeared painting shirt and threw it over her stool.

Rafe waited at the door for her to precede him. They walked back to the house across the grass, three feet separating them. Lexie put the kettle on automatically.

"I don't want anything to drink, thanks," Rafe said.

"I do." Lexie opened a tea canister and plunked a herbal teabag in a cup. She rarely drank hard liquor, and of course she wouldn't now that she was pregnant. But right this minute she wished she had a shot of scotch. "You should have called first."

"I wasn't sure you'd see me." He paused. "How are you?"

She pushed back her hair, her chin high. "Fine. My family has been great. Very supportive."

He flinched, telling her that her shot had hit home.

"*You* look like hell," she added, wanting to wound him.

His hand went automatically to his belly. "I'm fine."

Fine? She didn't think so. He needed a haircut and his stomach was obviously still hurting him. She got out another cup and dug around for a peppermint teabag. The silence stretched out, broken by the quiet roar of the water in the kettle as it heated.

Lexie turned away from him to tidy the counter Hetty had already cleaned. Every particle of her wanted to go into his arms, hear him whisper in her ear that everything was going to be okay.

"How's your mother?" Rafe asked. "Has she found another sex therapist?"

Lexie winced.

"Sorry," he said. "That was supposed to be funny."

"It wasn't." They were both wound up tight. "She and Dad are working on their problems."

"I saw my folks on the weekend," Rafe said.

"Where do they live again?" The mundane conversation felt surreal as they waited for the water to boil.

"Horsham, out in the Western District."

"I know where Horsham is." She poured water into the cups and handed him one. "I guess your dad is happy you got your boat."

"Yeah, he's happy about that." Rafe was looking down at his tea as though he didn't know what it was.

"Come into the living room." Lexie started for the couch then changed her mind and went to the dining table. She sat on the window side and gestured to the chair opposite.

Negotiating positions.

He'd made no attempt to touch her. And he'd better not. This visit of his was strictly business.

Rafe put his cup down and pulled out his wallet. He took a folded slip of paper and set it in front of her. "This is what I can afford at this time. I haven't checked what I owe by law. We can work that out later."

Lexie was tempted to snatch the check and run to the bank as fast as she could. Instead she pushed it back across the polished wood. "You don't have to pay support until the baby's born."

"Just take it. You need it."

Her curiosity got the better of her and she flipped the check over to read the amount—$5,000.

"How can you afford this?" she asked dully. "Didn't you just spend all your money on a boat?"

"Never mind that." He wrapped his hands around his china mug. "Make sure you put it in the bank," he added.

"I told you, I don't want your money." His fingers against the delicate china were long and well shaped; strong. She thought of her drawings...

"It's for the baby," he said, his jaw tight.

"No, it's not," she said. "It's for your conscience." Even as she told herself she despised him, she recalled how he'd eaten her watery two-minute noodles and pretended they were delicious.

"If you need to use it for...your own expenses, that's okay, too," he added.

"What happened with your boss after I left?" She had trouble meeting his gaze. "Were you fired?"

"I resigned first."

Her eyes widened. "But I thought you needed the job…"

"And by the way, thanks for choosing such an opportune moment to make your announcement. You have a real flair for drama."

She dropped her gaze—her timing *had* been unfair. But beneath the surface her humiliation burned. She was too old for him to have a relationship with but not to screw.

Rafe leaned forward. "Look, I have to ask you something. Please understand I'm not trying to offend or accuse you. But I need to know—" He broke off, apparently trying to word the question properly. "The thing is, we were only together a week. You don't know how long your IUD was missing."

It dawned on her what he was getting at. Her chest tightened painfully. She let go of her rattling cup and laid her trembling hands flat on the table, steadying herself. "I *do* know who I've slept with. And when. There's been no one else for six months." She leveled her gaze at him. "Like it or not, the baby is yours. However," she added coldly, "when the baby is born we can do a paternity test."

"Agreed. And if it turns out you're right, here's what I propose—" He broke off with a grimace. "Let me rephrase that. I provide material support— money—and you raise the child."

"I'll allow you as much access as you want—"

"I don't want it." His expression hardened. "I won't

be a father to the kid. I won't take it on the weekends or holidays. I won't teach little Jimmy to ride a bike or chauffeur little Julie to ballet class. I won't be part of his or her life."

She felt a spurt of anger. Deep down she'd hoped he would come around once he'd had time to get used to the idea of being a father. Not to marry her because she didn't want that, but to be a father to their child.

"I'm not asking for anything for myself," she said. "But how can you turn your back on your own flesh and blood?"

"I don't want this baby. I wouldn't be a good father." Shadows shifted in his dark eyes. "But I don't want to be a bad one, either. I don't want the kid to look at me and see resentment staring back at him."

Lexie stared at him, not comprehending how anyone could feel that way. "You don't give yourself much credit."

"You see, the thing is, I already resent it." Rafe's grip on his cup tightened, whitening the pads of his fingertips. "It's not the baby's fault he was conceived. But I don't have a job. Soon I'll have no home. I've bills to pay, responsibilities coming out of my yin yang."

"Yin yang," she said with a scoffing laugh. "Do you even know what that term means?"

"Oh, God. Not this New Age crap." He took a sip of his peppermint tea and made a face.

"Opposites," she told him even though he hadn't asked. "Light and dark. Hot and cold. Soft and hard. Morning and night…."

"Like us." Rafe dragged a hand over his face, then settled his chin in his palm. "We're opposites."

"We—" She broke off. A cramp caught her by surprise. She clutched her abdomen with both hands.

"What's wrong?" he said, sitting up straighter.

"I don't know." Another stabbing pain doubled her over.

"Are you…? What do you call it—miscarrying?" He got to his feet and started around the table toward her.

"What?" She couldn't believe he'd leaped so quickly to that conclusion. Had that really been a note of hope she'd heard in his voice? "You'd like that, wouldn't you? That would solve your problem."

"No, I meant—"

"I don't care what you meant." Bent at the waist, she backed away from him. "Get out of my house."

He pulled his phone out. "I'll call Emergency."

But even as he was punching in numbers, the cramp eased off. Slowly Lexie straightened. Waited another few seconds. "Never mind. It's gone. The pain is gone."

Rafe hesitated then clicked off his phone. "Are you sure?"

"I'm sure." Gathering up their cups, she glared at him. "And now you can leave."

CHAPTER TWELVE

LEXIE HELD HERSELF together until Rafe was gone. Trembling, she eased herself onto the couch and called the clinic.

"Come in right away," Bev, the receptionist, said when Lexie explained the situation. "Natalie will squeeze you in between patients. Is there any bleeding?"

"I...I had some spotting a week or so ago. Hang on." Lexie pulled up her skirt and checked. "Yes, I'm bleeding." A tremor rocked her voice. "Am I going to miscarry?"

"Dr. Higgins will be able to answer your questions," Bev said. "Just come in as soon as you can."

Lexie hung up and grabbed her purse. She slipped on her sandals. Then stopped dead.

The portrait. She still had to frame and crate it.

For a moment she wavered. The pain was gone....

No. What was she thinking? Spotting, cramps. She had to get checked out by the doctor.

Without any more delay she drove to the clinic. Bev called the nurse, who ushered Lexie into an empty examination room to lie down while she waited for Natalie.

Natalie came through the door in dark pants and a V-neck sweater. "How are you doing?" She slid her fingers around Lexie's wrist to check her pulse. While Lexie filled her in on what had been happening in halting words. Natalie released her wrist and squeezed her shoulder. "Get undressed and we'll see what's going on."

Lexie did as requested, checking her underwear, relieved to see there was no fresh blood. She told Natalie that when the doctor returned to do the examination.

Natalie confirmed what Sienna had told her previously and reassured her that it didn't necessarily mean she was miscarrying. "But I want you to take it easy for the next few days. Get plenty of rest. Lying down improves the blood flow to the uterus and helps the placenta attach itself more firmly."

Lexie gripped the sheet. "I don't have time to rest."

Natalie stripped off her latex gloves and disposed of them in the bin. "You want to do everything possible to keep your baby, don't you?"

"Of course I want to keep my baby." A tear seeped from the outer corner of her eye.

"Everything will be fine," Natalie reassured her, patting her arm. "Get dressed and we'll talk some more."

A few minutes later Lexie sat in the chair next to the doctor's desk, twisting a tissue in her hands. Her breath hitched. "I—I'm not sure if this has anything to do with the cramping but it happened after I'd been on my feet painting for several hours."

"As I said, it's better if you rest," Natalie told her. "But miscarriages generally aren't caused by anything the mother does, or doesn't do. Don't blame yourself."

"And then I was talking to the father," Lexie went on. She heard what Natalie was saying but it was hard not to try to think of reasons this could be happening to her. "It was pretty stressful. He's not interested in having a role in bringing up the baby. I'm going to be doing this on my own."

"But you're not alone," Natalie assured her. "You've got your family. Do they know?"

"I told them. The reaction is…mixed. But you're right, they are supportive."

Natalie studied Lexie. "Your situation isn't ideal but you're usually so calm and upbeat. Is anything bothering you? Anything else you want to talk to me about?"

"I'm okay," Lexie said with a small shrug. "Working too hard."

Natalie hesitated then said gently, "This isn't your first pregnancy, is it?" She waited. Lexie didn't reply. "I can tell, you know. Do you want to talk about it?"

Lexie reached for another tissue. No, she didn't want to talk about it.

But...Natalie was her doctor. And if the information could help this baby... "I—I had an abortion when I was seventeen."

"How far along were you?"

"Twelve weeks," she said in a small voice.

Natalie glanced at her with compassion. "Lexie, I'm not judging you. Twelve weeks is a little late but lots of young girls don't even realize they're pregnant at first."

Lexie didn't reply to that. "Are you sure my baby is all right?"

"To give you peace of mind I'll order a sonogram." Natalie reached for a blank request form and scrawled a few words. "Get this done as soon as possible. The sonographer can check the placenta attachment. When you see your baby's heartbeat you'll feel a lot better."

RAFE WAS HEADING east on the freeway, halfway home to Sassafras when his conscience started bothering him. He shouldn't have left Lexie like that, even if she'd ordered him to go.

He may not care about the baby, but *she* did.

She had family and friends, he told himself.

But he'd been there when she'd felt the cramping.

Rafe had his phone connected to the hands-free

car set and Lexie's number on speed dial. He hit a few buttons and waited while it rang. No answer. Could she have gone to the hospital? He didn't know a damn thing about pregnancy. What if the pain turned out to be serious?

And then there was her Archibald Prize portrait. She'd talked about crating it and having it shipped to Sydney. It would be just like her to try to lift a heavy framed canvas and strain a gasket.

Face it, he wasn't going to feel good until he made certain she was all right. He put on his indicator and took the next exit, crossed the overpass and got back on the freeway heading south again.

Now he felt a sense of urgency. The speedometer climbed to the maximum speed limit and beyond. Where would she be? He didn't have her brother or sister's phone numbers. Anyway, they'd be at work—

The doctor. If Lexie was worried she would have gone to the clinic to get checked out.

Rafe got the number of the Summerside Medical Clinic from directory assistance and made the call. He explained the situation to the receptionist, a woman named Bev.

"Lexie was in to see Dr. Higgins a short time ago," Bev admitted cautiously. "She's not here now."

Relief and fear washed over Rafe simultaneously. "Is she all right? Is her baby okay?"

"I can't give out information about patients," Bev said.

Rafe thumped the steering wheel. "I'm asking because..." Damn, this was hard to say. "My name is Rafe Ellersley. I'm the father."

"Why didn't you say so!" Bev's manner became warmer. "When she left here she was going to get a sonogram in Frankston. I called ahead for her. They said they could squeeze her in at two o'clock."

Rafe glanced at his watch. It was 1:45 p.m. If he didn't hit any road construction or traffic accidents he could make it. He got the address of the diagnostic center from Bev. "Thanks. I'll head straight there."

Twenty minutes later he pulled into the parking lot. Instead of getting out of his car, he sat paralyzed with indecision.

Lexie might get the wrong idea if he went charging in there. Might think he'd changed his mind, that he was ready to act like a father.

To hell with it. He flung himself out of the car and slammed the door, locking it with the remote as he hurried inside. He found the ultrasound department and pushed through the frosted glass door. Lexie was sitting on the brown vinyl couch, drinking from a plastic cup.

She lowered the cup, her fingers indenting the soft plastic. "What are you doing here?"

He took a seat beside her. Stopped himself from touching her shoulder, her knee. "Are you okay?"

"I guess." Her eyes were wide, frightened. "There was some bleeding."

"That doesn't sound good." He felt awkward, not sure what he was doing here.

"My doctor isn't too worried. But she thought I should get it checked out just to be sure." She glanced at her watch. "I hope they hurry. They made me drink a gallon of water."

The nurse, a middle-aged brunette in a pale green uniform, appeared in the doorway next to the reception desk. "Lexie Thatcher? You can come in now."

Lexie rose, glancing back at him.

"Your partner can come in, too," the nurse told her, smiling. "The dads love this."

"He's not—" She broke off, glancing at him in confusion. Because of course, he was the dad.

"I'll wait out here," Rafe said.

"Come on in," the nurse encouraged him with a wave of her hand. "You'll regret it afterward if you don't see the first images of your baby."

Rafe met Lexie's gaze. She shrugged. Reluctantly he got up and followed her. The nurse led them to a small room dominated by a narrow bed and an ultrasound machine much like the one they'd used on his wrist when he'd injured it playing football.

He sat on a chair out of the way while Lexie lay down. Following instructions, she pulled up her top and unzipped her skirt, tugging it over her still nearly flat stomach to her hips.

Rafe eyed the dip of her waist, her smooth bare skin, and the gentle flare of her hips. He swallowed and glanced away. He didn't have any right to look.

The sonographer, a slim dark-skinned woman in her thirties, came into the room. "Hi, I'm Celine." She smiled as she squirted gel onto Lexie. "Is this your first pregnancy?"

"N- Y-yes," Lexie said.

Rafe cocked his head at her slight hesitation.

"No," she amended. "That is, I was pregnant once, years ago but…it didn't go to term."

Rafe started. It was a reminder of how little he knew about Lexie. Questions flowed through his mind. What happened to the baby? Was that why she wanted this one so badly?

"Don't be nervous. The procedure is completely safe." Celine glanced over the doctor's request form then set it aside. "You've been having some bleeding?"

"Yes. Twice now."

Rafe's head came up. Twice?

"You'll need to take it easy when you leave here. But I'm sure your doctor told you that."

Celine clicked buttons with her left hand while, with her right, she guided the transducer over Lexie's abdomen. She went silent, concentrating on the monitor in front of her. "How far along are you?"

"About nine weeks."

"Ah, that's why I'm having trouble finding— There's the little rascal. See him?"

Rafe cleared his throat, curious despite himself. "So, you can tell it's a boy?"

Celine chuckled as she pressed into Lexie's belly with the transducer. "No, that's just a figure of speech. But look there, you can see the heartbeat."

"Oh!" Lexie's voice caught. "Rafe, come and see."

Grudgingly, he got up and stood behind her, looking to where the arrow pointed. Inside the ever-shifting outline of a rounded body topped by an outsize head was a pulsating dot. Just a blip on the screen, really.

He made the mistake of glancing at Lexie. She was watching him, her eyes shining. Rafe felt a jolt run through him clear down to the soles of his feet.

It was nothing to do with the baby, he told himself. That was just the effect she had on him.

His palms sweating, he glanced back at the screen. The heartbeat was rapid but steady. This speck of life had come into existence because of him and Lexie. He couldn't get his head around it.

All of a sudden he couldn't bear being here another second, seeing Lexie's excitement. Not knowing what he was feeling. All he'd wanted to do was make sure Lexie was okay, not take part in this…this prebirth bonding ritual. "I'll wait outside."

"Rafe?" Lexie said.

As he was shutting the door behind him, he heard Celine say, "Don't worry. Some of the dads get queasy. I'll check the placenta attachment now."

Rafe walked straight through the reception area and down the main corridor, pushing through to the parking lot. He sucked in a lungful of air. Until a few minutes ago the baby hadn't felt real. He'd thought he could just pay a monthly bill, like a direct debit on his car loan, to cover expenses and that would be it.

It was only genetic material that linked him and that blip on the screen. DNA, like the molecules floating in the background of Sienna's portrait. It was purely biological; not emotional. He started to walk so he wouldn't feel it tugging at him.

Lexie was carrying his baby.

He got in his car and pulled out of the parking lot in a screech of tires. Perspiration dampened his scalp and he flexed his hands on the wheel.

Sometimes you don't know what you want until it happens.

Bullshit. He didn't like babies.

He came to an intersection and put on his indicator to take the turn toward the freeway and home. He'd seen Lexie, eased his conscience and his mind.

But it wasn't over. She still had that painting to deal with. Rafe thumped the steering wheel once with his fist. That was *her* problem. He should be updating his résumé, looking for another job.

The light changed to green. He sighed. There was really no decision to be made. He changed his indicator from left to right, checked his rearview mirror and ignoring the blare of a car horn behind him, eased into the next lane of traffic and made a U-turn.

He pulled up in front of the diagnostic center and parked just as she came out. He might never have gone anywhere for all she knew. For a moment she paused there in her filmy skirt and scoop-necked top. Her collarbone stood out as she turned her head, searching for her car. She looked frail, he thought, and without warning protectiveness swept over him.

He rejected that with a snort. She was frail like a Ninja. And she didn't want him.

He opened his car door and got out. "Lexie!"

She walked over, moving slowly. "I thought you'd run off."

"I— It was a bit close in there. Is everything all right? Is the placenta attached to whatever it's supposed to be attached to?"

"Yes. I'm supposed to rest for a few days."

"What about your painting?"

"I'll call Jack, see if he can help me."

Rafe glanced across the parking lot. He jammed his hands in his back pockets. "I'll do it," he said gruffly.

Her gaze narrowed. "Is this guilt? I don't want any part of that."

He liked her. That hadn't changed when she'd gotten pregnant. Or when she threw him out.

Or called him immature.

With a shrug, he said, "I've got nothing better to do."

LEXIE PARKED in her driveway, leaving room to get at the back wall of the carport where her painting crates were stored. She closed her eyes and slumped against the headrest, just for a minute until Rafe arrived. Sleep was overtaking her when she heard the sound of his car. Glancing in the rearview mirror, she felt a trickle of relief as he pulled in behind her. She'd half expected him not to show up.

She'd been surprised to see him at the sonogram center. And shocked when he'd actually come in with her. The expression on his face when he first saw the baby's heartbeat… She'd thought for a moment he might have felt something, been struck by the miracle of the baby growing inside her. Then he'd taken to his heels, clearly scared witless by the enormity of it all.

The responsibility.

She shook off the disappointment. How many times could she put herself through this with him?

Fatigue dragged at her but she put her game face on. The placenta was in place, the baby was developing. Once she got the painting framed, crated and shipped, then she could rest.

Rafe parked at the curb in front of her house. He got out of his car and came down to the carport. "Do we have to build a crate? Should I go get wood?"

"I've got one," she said, nodding at the shallow wooden box, six foot by five foot, against the back wall of the carport. "If you could carry it to the studio for me, that would be great."

Rafe half carried, half dragged the crate across the lawn. He averted his gaze as he passed the trampoline. Was that where she'd conceived, Lexie wondered.

"It would be easier if I took one end," she said when he paused for a breather. "It's not only heavy, it's awkward to carry."

"Forget it." He picked it up again, broad shoulders stretched, biceps taut beneath his short-sleeved shirt.

A warm tingling sensation stole through her. Even though she was pregnant. Even though they'd broken up. Even though she was dead on her feet. She was still attracted to him. As much, if not more, than before. But where once she would have run her hands over his shoulders, felt the firmness of his muscles, coaxed him into bed…now all she could do was issue directions.

"Lean it against the wall for now," she said as he turned sideways to take it through the studio door. "I have to frame the painting before we can crate it."

Crossing to the opposite side of the studio, she

started to pull a large gilt frame from a stack of frames resting against the wall.

"Go sit down," he said, edging her away. He'd worked up a sheen of perspiration and smelled of warm male.

"I'll get the matting," she said, moving reluctantly. From the long, slotted cabinet at the back of the studio she brought sheets of mat board in burgundy and olive-green and laid them on the table. Then she gathered her tools—a long metal straight edge, mat cutter, fine sandpaper, soft pencil and linen tape. She fixed him with a defiant stare. "I have to do the matting. It takes skill and practice."

Rafe brought over a wooden stool. "Sit as much as possible. And tell me if you feel any cramping." He glanced at the painting. "Is it dry?"

"It's tacky in spots but I can't wait any longer. It's due at the Sydney gallery tomorrow."

She measured and cut the mat board to size, methodically yet swiftly, her movements efficient through long practice. While she worked she issued instructions to Rafe, at the other end of the table, to get the glass and place it into the frame. She'd had that specially cut months ago when she'd first started working on the portrait.

They'd been working in silence for some minutes when Rafe said, "When you were cramping earlier, you didn't tell me that you'd had spotting before."

"I talked to Sienna. She told me it was common. Not to worry about it."

"And you never mentioned you'd been pregnant before."

She'd wondered if he'd picked up on that. "We haven't exactly been having heart-to-heart conversations lately. I didn't think you'd be interested. And frankly…" She glanced at him. "It's none of your business."

"Maybe not," he said. "But I want to know. How old were you?"

Her hands started to tremble. She had to put down the cutter for fear of nicking the mat board. "There's not much to tell. I was seventeen."

He was silent a moment. "Did you have an abortion?"

"I…" She drew in a deep breath. "Yes."

"Is that why this baby is so important to you?"

The child was her second chance. A shot at redemption. She hadn't fully acknowledged that until this very moment.

Feeling tears burning the backs of her eyes, she blinked and glanced away. "All babies are important."

"Did that father run out on you, too?"

She tried to make light of it. "You think you're too young to be a father. That guy still had pimples." She touched the heels of her hands to her eyes, hating that her hormones made her weepy. That Rafe still had the power to make her feel. "I don't want to dwell on the past. Let's get this done, okay?"

Finished with the glass, he held the mat board steady for her while she cut the long beveled edge. Next she sandpapered it lightly then got Rafe to bring the portrait to the table. She positioned the double layers and taped them with linen tape. Then she lowered the matted canvas into the frame and secured a thin sheet of fiberboard backing with metal flanges.

"Done!" she said, straightening. "Can you put it back on the easel? I'd like to savor the finished painting for a moment before we pack it away."

Rafe lifted and placed it on the easel then stepped back beside Lexie. She studied the portrait critically, seeing tiny things she wished she'd done differently. It was always that way. But overall she was pleased.

"It's amazing," Rafe said.

"Yeah, thanks," she replied. Her back was aching and now that she'd stopped working she noticed a heavy feeling in her groin. All she wanted to do was lie down. But she had to push on. "Now to pack it."

Rafe hoisted the crate onto the table and went back for the sheet of plywood that formed the lid. He leaned it against the wall and studied the scars of old postal stickers and address labels. "It's like a well-traveled suitcase."

"I'm going to sit down for a minute," she said, suddenly feeling breathless. "In the cupboard there are sheets of high-density foam. Get them and line the crate." She found a straight back chair and lowered herself gingerly. A cramp ripped through her abdomen. With a gasp, she bent over, her elbows on her knees.

Rafe spun around. "Are you all right?"

"Fine," she said tightly, waving him away. "Just get the foam."

Giving her a worried glance, he did as she asked. A few minutes later he said, "I've lined the crate. Now what?"

Lexie lifted her head with an effort. "Put the painting on top of the foam and pack more foam around the sides and over top. Then…" She broke off to gasp. "Then put the lid on and screw it down."

He was at her side in an instant, taking her arm to help her up. "Go inside and lie down. I can finish this."

She tugged her arm away. "I want to see it through." She met his gaze and nodded at the painting. "That's my baby, too."

Rafe hesitated, then he nodded. "All right."

He went back to the crate and fitted a screw into the preformed holes. When he'd tightened the last screw and the label was affixed to the lid, Lexie rose and walked slowly back to the house. The heaviness in her belly had increased. Something didn't feel right.

She eased herself onto her bed with an involuntary

moan and shut her eyes, feeling more tired than she'd ever felt in her life. In the living room she could hear Rafe call the freight company that specialized in artworks and arrange for the crate to be picked up and shipped overnight to Sydney.

Then he was standing in her doorway. "May I come in?"

She nodded weakly and closed her eyes. "Thank you for everything. I'll be fine now."

Rafe walked to the bed and sat on the edge. It sank beneath his weight. She felt him brush her hair off her forehead. "Lexie?"

She opened her eyes. "Yes, Rafe?"

"I think we should get married."

A blossom of hope unfurled in her heart. *Not just sex, but love.*

And then the moment passed.

What was she thinking? That's not why he was asking.

CHAPTER THIRTEEN

RAFE COULDN'T believe he'd asked her to marry him.
The words had just come out. One minute he'd been
thinking about asking if she wanted a cup of tea.
Then without warning, he'd blurted out an offer of
the next fifty years of his life.

"What did you say?" Her eyes were half-closed; a
frown wrinkled her forehead. "I don't think I heard
you properly."

He took her hand. It felt hot. He pressed the back
of his other hand to her forehead. That was hot,
too.

He cleared his throat. "I said, will you marry
me?"

Her eyes opened wide. "Rafe, don't be silly."

"Why is it silly? I want to do the right thing."

"That's…exactly what's wrong…with your pro-
posal." She spoke slowly, as if every word was an
effort. "You don't love me. You're only asking me
out of a sense of duty, of responsibility."

"No…"

"Would you be asking me this if it wasn't for the
baby?"

"How can I answer that? There *is* a baby." He rubbed her cold fingers, flaking off a bit of dried paint. "We could be good together."

"Being sexually compatible isn't the same as being committed partners over a lifetime."

"Granted but…but how do you know I don't love you?"

"You haven't said so, for one thing. And even if you said it now," she added, forestalling his next words, "how could I ever believe you?"

Rafe got up and paced the narrow space at the foot of the bed. "You need to be looked after. I *do* feel a sense of responsibility. To you and our child. I don't have much to offer right now but…" His mouth ticked up at one corner. "We'll never want for fresh fish."

He'd been trying to make her laugh. She just gazed at him wearily.

Picking up a bottle of perfume from her dresser, he held the crystal stopper to his nose. The light floral scent brought the night of the barbecue flooding back. "I want to marry a woman who makes love on a trampoline."

"And I don't care if I get married or not."

"Then we'll live together. I'm not hung up on pieces of paper. At least think about it."

She shook her head. "I have thought. Every time I get tempted I remind myself that when you're forty, I'll be fifty-two. Men have their midlife crises at that age. They have affairs, get divorced, run off with the nanny. All those things would be so much more likely if your wife was twelve years older."

"I'll buy a sports car instead, I promise."

That got a smile from her. But at the same time a tear slipped from the corner of her eye. "No."

Rafe paced some more, pushing fist into palm as if he could force the two of them together. "Marriage requires a leap of faith, regardless of age or circumstance." He came around the foot of the bed and sat down again. "There are no guarantees, even for people of similar age, temperament and interests."

"Exactly. That's why a couple has to give themselves a fighting chance for the marriage to survive."

Rafe reached for her hand again and twined his fingers with hers. He gazed down at their interlocked hands. "I threw away my career for you. That ought to tell you something."

"You're an idiot?" When he frowned she squeezed his hand. "Oh, Rafe, I'm only joking. You're young and handsome and smart and funny. Someday you'll meet a woman your own age. When the time is right you'll have children." She glanced away and added quietly, "Children you want."

That hurt him, a well-deserved shaft of pain. His motives for asking her to marry him were muddy, he knew that. But it felt like the right thing to do.

As if she'd read his mind, she glanced back to him.

"People don't get married these days just because there's a baby on the way."

"Some do."

She shook her head. "Asking someone to marry you should be what you *want* to do, not what you *should* do."

A spasm made her face twist. With another deep breath her skin smoothed again but now her features were stretched tight. "I'm all jumbled up from so many things happening to me at once. We're different, not just in age but in everything. I'm not sure *I* could love *you*."

Rafe blinked. Maybe it was egotistical on his part but he'd thought—he'd assumed—that given half a chance she would love him. "I—I don't understand. Are you saying—"

"Thank you for your help today," she whispered. "Maybe you should go." She rolled onto her side and curled into a fetal position. Her eyes shut tightly and two creases formed between her eyebrows.

"Lexie," he said, alarmed. "Are you all right? I'm going to call the doctor."

"I'm…fine." Another spasm gripped her, contorting her face and twisting her body beneath the blankets.

"Lexie!"

The doorbell rang.

"The shipping company," she gasped. "Go. Answer it."

Rafe hesitated. The doorbell rang again. He hurried down the hallway and opened the door. A reddish-haired man with a deep dimple in his chin stood there, an identification tag around his neck and a clipboard in his hand. "Pickup for Ms. Lexie Thatcher?"

"Around the back," Rafe said. "Have you got a dolly? It's heavy." He glanced about for his shoes and remembered he'd left them at the back door. He led the way through the carport in his sock feet. "This will be delivered to Sydney tomorrow, won't it?"

"Guaranteed by noon tomorrow." The man wheeled the dolly across the grass.

Rafe opened the studio door and then helped the man load the crate onto the dolly. "Careful. It's a framed painting. There's glass."

They went back across the lawn, through the carport and up the ramp into the back of the freight truck. Rafe signed the docket and took the receipt. Before the truck had pulled out of the driveway he was hurrying back inside.

"Lexie, the painting's on its way. You made the deadline." He paused in the doorway of her bedroom. Beneath the covers she was still curled into a tight ball. "Lexie?"

Her face was white as she turned to him. "Call my doctor."

Rafe crossed the room in swift strides. He felt her forehead. It was clammy now. Gently he prised back the covers. His stomach tipped into a queasy free fall.

The sheets were soaked with blood.

LEXIE WOKE UP in a hospital bed. A saline drip was inserted into the back of her left hand, the needle taped to her skin. She glanced about, dazed. Renita was asleep in a chair next to the bed, her hair tousled and her blue blouse slipping off her shoulder.

Across the ward, an elderly lady was snoring. The clock on the wall read 3:45. Was that a.m. or p.m.? The lights were dim and it was quiet. She thought it must be early.

She instinctively clutched at her stomach. Had she miscarried? She could feel a bulky sanitary pad between her legs. Presumably that meant she was still bleeding.

This was all her fault. She hadn't listened to her doctor. Instead of going to bed and resting like a sensible person she'd been on her feet for an hour or more to frame her painting.

Where was Rafe?

Would his offer still stand if she lost her baby?

Panic overtook her. *What if she lost her baby?*

"Renita." Lexie stretched out a hand and touched her sister's knee with her fingertips.

Renita came awake with a start. She reached for her glasses on the bedside table, then scooted her chair forward. "How are you feeling?" her sister asked, taking her hand.

She clung to Renita. "What's happening to my baby? Am I still pregnant?"

"Oh, sweetie. The doctors don't know. They have to wait till morning to do a sonogram to try to find the fetal heartbeat."

Lexie fell back on her pillow. "It's my fault."

"Don't blame yourself," Renita whispered. "Natalie, Sienna, they both said it's not from anything you did."

She hadn't rested when they told her to. How could she not blame herself? "Is Rafe...?"

"Rafe was wonderful. He called Sienna, then Hetty. He stuck around for hours. Then he had to go home to his dog. Said he was only renting and if the carpet was ruined he'd wouldn't get his bond back."

"Poor Murphy. I wonder how long he'd been cooped up." She pressed fingers to her lips. "Yin and Yang!"

"They're taken care of. Don't worry. Just rest. Natalie said she'd be back first thing in the morning. Sienna's going to be here for your sonogram." Renita started to rise. "Do you want water? Cup of tea?"

"No, thank you. Please sit. I need to talk to you." Lexie smoothed the rumpled top sheet. "Rafe asked me to marry him."

Renita's tired face lit for a moment before her expression turned cautious. "What did you say?"

"No, of course."

"Why, Lexie? He's young but, gee, I think he's a keeper."

"He only asked me out of a…a sense of duty or something. I don't want to marry him just because I'm pregnant. He'd be bound to end up resenting me. And the baby."

"You can't be sure about that," Renita said, troubled. "If he cares about you he'd come to love the baby, too. And now that he's had a chance to think—"

"You didn't hear the things he was saying when I first told him I was pregnant. I trust a gut reaction far more than a reasoned response." She shook her head sadly. "I'm still romantic enough to want to marry for love."

"I guess I wouldn't want to marry someone in these circumstances, either," Renita conceded. "How do *you* feel about *him?*"

Lexie fell silent, studying the ceiling. Rafe was energy and heat, a shining life force. He was the light that filled the crystal. "I could love him."

"Then don't make up your mind to refuse him now." Renita yawned. "You've been through too much. You need to rest."

"You should go home, too," Lexie said. "I feel terrible having caused all this trouble."

"Don't be silly." Renita rose and stretched her back out. "But I do have to work tomorrow." She blinked sleepily at the clock. "I mean, today." She kissed Lexie on the cheek. "I'll come back later this afternoon—if you're still here. Try to get more sleep."

Sleep was impossible. Lexie lay awake, tormented by guilt and doubt. What kind of a mother would she make if she always put painting before her child? Maybe she'd been right when she'd told Rafe she wasn't destined to have a child. Twenty-one years ago she'd aborted one baby to pursue her art. Now the universe was punishing her.

But she loved children so much. The vision of her own baby was pure and clear. A little girl, a boy; it didn't matter. She wanted to teach him or her to finger paint, to collect pebbles and shells, to see beauty in the veins of a leaf and clouds in the sky. She wanted to cuddle her baby, warm and soft and so alive….

Lexie closed her eyes. She turned her face into the pillow. She was so very tired….

RAFE WALKED through the hospital corridors, past orderlies wheeling trolleys and a pair of doctors in scrubs. It was six in the morning and the nurses were starting to make their rounds. He slowed outside Lexie's ward and peeked in. The light was on over her elderly roommate's empty bed, the covers thrown back. He entered quietly and stood at the foot of Lexie's bed. Even in sleep, she looked exhausted.

He wasn't much better. He'd been up most of the night, catching only a couple hours of shut-eye at home before racing back to the hospital. He felt the strain in his cold, tense muscles, in the headache from lack of sleep. His stomach was a tight ball of pain.

Where was the nurse? Who could he ask about Lexie's condition? And the baby—had she miscarried or not? He picked up her chart hanging off the end of the bed and scanned the pages. There was nothing here that told him what he wanted to know, not that he could decipher anyway.

Rafe walked back to the door to look out into the corridor. No one was at the nurses' station. He heard a sound and glanced over his shoulder.

Lexie opened her eyes. "Rafe?"

He was at her side quickly, lowering himself into the chair, leaning toward the bed. "How are you feeling?"

She turned her head to face him. "Tired. Achey."

"The baby...?"

"The bleeding hasn't stopped." Her eyes, huge and shadowed, searched his face. "They won't know if the baby is alive until they do another sonogram."

Taking Lexie's hand he lifted it to his mouth and held her gaze over her small paint-stained knuckles. Lowering her hand, he kept it tucked in his. "When will that be?"

"This morning." She made an attempt to smile. "How's Murphy? Did he ruin the carpet?"

"I'll have to call Guinness Books. He may have set the world's record on bladder control." When her smile faded, he added, "I'm sure everything will be fine. They'll find the heartbeat, then you'll be out of danger."

The fine lines at the corners of her eyes tightened. She gripped his fingers. "Even if I don't miscarry I...I don't think I'm cut out to be a mother. I'm disorganized, selfish with my time—"

"Lexie, stop. You're too hard on yourself."

"No, listen," she insisted. "This is real. When I'm working I forget everything else. Nothing else matters but finishing the painting. The poor kid would be neglected. As much as I love children, I—I don't trust myself to be a good parent."

"Don't talk about it now," he said. "You're not thinking clearly. You've got hormones and...and worry over taxes and the Archibald. All of it together is messing up your brain."

The elderly woman from the other bed shuffled in with a damp towel over her arm and her toiletries bag in hand. Her thin gray hair was newly washed and plastered to her scalp. Slowly, she draped her towel over the back of a chair and put her toiletry bag away in a cupboard. She sat on the bed to catch her breath.

A middle-aged nurse with short brown hair and glasses on a chain around her neck entered the ward, pushing a trolley loaded with Dixie cups of pills and a bottle of water.

"Good morning, ladies," she said, cheerfully. "Let me help you, Mrs. Mitchell. Up you go." She assisted the older woman back into bed then poured a glass of water for her to take her medication with.

Rafe stepped back when the nurse came to Lexie's bed. She rearranged the pillows, clucking briskly over her. "We'll do your observations then I'll take you downstairs for the sonogram." She popped a thermometer under Lexie's tongue and strapped on the blood pressure cuff.

Hetty arrived and touched Rafe's arm. "What's happening?"

"She's going for a sonogram in a few minutes."

An orderly arrived wheeling a gurney. He and the nurse transferred Lexie from her bed.

"Come with me," Lexie said to Rafe and her mother as the nurse began to push the gurney.

"Of course." Hetty took her hand.

Rafe followed, his steps lagging as they walked the long corridor to the elevator. They rode down two floors and walked along another endless corridor around so many corners he lost track of where he was. This all felt unreal to him. How had he come to be in a hospital with this woman he liked a lot but barely knew, having tests on a baby neither of them had planned on? And only one of them wanted?

This is life, buddy. Shit happens.

The sonographer, a young Asian woman with a pink barrette in her hair, pushed the transducer across Lexie's abdomen. Hetty stood at her side, keeping a death grip on her hand.

Sienna arrived and stood behind her head, her hands resting on Lexie's shoulders. "Natalie couldn't make it but she'll be in later."

Rafe stood back, feeling out of place. Everyone was transfixed by the screen. He was watching Lexie's face. Tearstained and pale, desperately searching for that tiny pulse of light.

Of life.

Minutes passed. The tension became unbearable.

"There's the embryonic sac," the sonographer said. She moved the scanner, pressing deeply into Lexie's abdomen. Her mouth tightened and she gave an almost imperceptible shake of her head.

"What's happening?" Lexie cried wildly. "Is the baby there? Someone tell me what's going on."

Rafe closed his eyes briefly. A dreadful silence had fallen over the room.

The sonographer glanced at Sienna, her expression grim. "It's empty."

"I'm so sorry, sweetie." Sienna bent to hug Lexie.

Rafe heard Lexie give a keening cry and collapse into stifled sobs. The sonographer quietly wiped the gel off Lexie's stomach and left the room. Hetty and

Sienna gathered around Lexie, holding her, trying to soothe her. Everyone was crying.

Rafe's heart was racing, his palms sweating. It hurt him to see Lexie so distraught. He felt guilty because he wasn't more upset.

Chiefly he felt…

Relief.

An enormous burden had been lifted from his shoulders. The pressure was off. He didn't have to try to be someone he wasn't. Or do things he wasn't ready for.

He was a bastard to feel this way. Lexie was sobbing as if her own life was coming to an end. He wanted to comfort her but the women were around her, their bodies like a shield, excluding him.

Rafe slipped out the door. He had to get out of here before someone noticed he wasn't grieving.

Lexie let herself into her house after two days in the hospital. The living room was bathed in honey-gold afternoon light. Yin and Yang leaped off the furniture and came running to greet her, their tails straight up in the air. They twined around her legs, purring loudly.

"Hello, my darlings." She crouched to pet them, gently butting first a cream then a chocolate head. "I hope Renita hasn't spoiled you too much. I know she feeds you canned tuna when I'm not home."

Hetty had dropped Lexie off at home and wanted

to come in but Lexie had told her she was tired. The truth was, she needed to be alone with her pain.

But although she was long used to living alone, as she walked through the living room and into the kitchen, the house felt empty. Grief went ahead of her, permeating the atmosphere.

She was empty. Her baby was gone.

The doorbell rang.

She thought about ignoring it, pretending she wasn't home. But it might be a neighbor, someone who saw her come in. She went to open the door.

Rafe stood there. Heartbreakingly, hatefully handsome.

He'd disappeared after the ultrasound and hadn't returned to the hospital. He'd sent a card and flowers. But he hadn't come in person.

She started to shut the door. He wedged his foot between the door and the jamb. "You've got to stop doing that," he said.

She yanked open the door and retreated to the living room. "What do you want?"

"To see you. See how you're doing."

"How do you think I'm doing?" Right now she was struggling to hold herself together. She would have whole minutes at a time when she was fine, then she would remember she'd lost her baby and the edges of her control would fray.

"I'm sorry I ran out after the ultrasound." He followed her, hands stuffed in his pockets. "You had

Hetty and Sienna. There was no room for a guy who—"

"Who'd never wanted to be there in the first place," she finished for him.

"Who wasn't a father. Or husband. Or boyfriend." His shoulders rose and fell. "I had no role. I was just a guy you'd slept with."

She turned away so he wouldn't see her hurt. She'd never been good about hiding her feelings. Since the miscarriage she'd felt raw, her emotions an open wound. Now she wanted to lash out at him just because he was there, because only a few short months ago he'd inspired joy and creativity in her.

She walked over to the dining table, sifted through some old mail and papers. Found his check. "Here," she said, holding it out to him. "Is this what you came for?"

He flinched, as if she'd slapped his face. "Keep it. You're going to need it."

She let it flutter back to the table. If he was going to be that foolish, let him. She sat on the couch and pulled a flowered cushion over her lap. "Well, you've seen me. I'm alive. You've appeased your conscience. You can go now."

Instead he lowered himself into the chintz-covered chair opposite the couch. "I also wanted to say I'm sorry for...for your loss."

"You sound like a funeral director. It was *your* loss, too, Rafe." She could hear the edge to her voice.

"Although I know you don't see it that way. You were probably relieved."

"Hey, I tried to step up to the plate but you didn't want me. You kept pushing me away."

"I wish—" She broke off. There was no point wishing. For anything.

Yang uncurled from his cushion at the end of the couch and padded over to her for a pat. Lexie shut her eyes and pressed her cheek against his soft fur. Her mood swings were no doubt from the hormones still circulating in her body but that didn't make them easier to bear.

"Did…did the doctor have any idea what caused the miscarriage?" Rafe asked.

"No. But I've seen the statistics. Women my age have a twenty-five percent chance of miscarrying." In just two years that figure would jump to fifty percent. "I should have been resting, not working. If I'd listened to my doctor…"

"I've done some research, too. There must have been something wrong with the baby's development. It's Nature's way."

She could feel the tears at the back of her eyes and willed them not to spill. "Don't you dare say it's probably better this way," she whispered.

"I would never say that." He shook his head. "Never. I know how much you wanted the baby."

Silence filled the space between them. Yang butted her chin to stroke him. Lexie kept her eyes closed, wishing despite everything that Rafe would cross the gap between the chair and the couch and put his arms around her; tell her everything was going to be all right.

"Okay, you're right." Rafe got to his feet, took a few steps, then spun back. "I admit it, I *was* relieved."

"You'd better go," she said, shoving Yang aside more roughly than she intended. "I don't need to hear this."

"*Listen.* You think I don't know how selfish that is? What an asshole that makes me? I'm trying to be honest here so that you'll believe me when I tell you other things."

She waited. What else could he possibly say?

"Relief isn't the only thing I feel. I'm also sorry for your sake you lost the baby." His dark eyes met hers. "*Desperately* sorry. You would make a great mother."

He startled a laugh out of her, accompanied by more tears. "Me? I'll never be a mother."

"Lexie, don't," he pleaded. "This is what I'm trying to get at. Don't punish yourself for the rest of your life because you had an abortion when you were seventeen."

She grabbed the pillow again and clutched it to her stomach. "How can you say that to me?"

"There isn't some cosmic conspiracy against you because you chose to terminate a pregnancy when you were young and ill equipped to cope with a baby."

"You've got it all wrong," she whispered. "That's not what I think."

"Isn't it?" He looked sad.

She got up and pushed past him, walking swiftly down the hall to her bedroom. She lay on the bed, her face pressed into the pillow, shoulders heaving with sobs.

A moment later, she heard the sound of the front door as it shut behind him.

CHAPTER FOURTEEN

"HEY, MOM." As he spoke into the phone, Rafe pulled books off the shelf with his one hand and packed them into a box at his feet. His living room was half-empty, packed boxes and furniture pushed to one side, waiting to go into storage.

"Rafe, it's nice to hear from you," Ellen exclaimed. "How is Lexie, and the baby?"

"Not good." He paused to take a breath. "She… miscarried."

He dropped his dictionary into a box with a thud. His relief over the miscarriage had been short-lived. He kept telling himself it had worked out for the best. But the loss of the baby had packed a wallop far greater than he'd expected. He wasn't grieving really; he was just…numb.

"I'm so sorry," Ellen said softly. "How is Lexie taking it?"

"She's…upset." Rafe dragged out another box and started loading his CD collection. They were practically antiques now that most of his music was on his MP3 player.

"And *you,* Rafe? You weren't happy about the prospect of being a father but…"

He stared at the CD cover in his hand, not even remembering the band or when he had bought it. "I'm not sure what I feel. Kind of empty, I guess. But then, I've also lost my job. Now I'm moving out of my house."

"Where are you going?" In the background he could hear the familiar sounds of her cooking dinner. The soft clang of pots hitting the stove element, water running.

"I'm moving onto my boat. In fact, I'd like you and Dad to come out fishing with me."

"Gee, I'm not sure. It's a long way to drive…."

"Come for the weekend. We can all stay on the boat."

She didn't reply right away. He felt his eyes burning and pressed two fingers to the bridge of his nose. "Please try to make it, Mum. I'd like to take Dad fishing."

If he couldn't be a good father, he could at least be a better son.

"WELCOME." Rafe greeted his parents around noon beneath the palm trees bordering the marina parking lot and led the way along the wharf to where his boat was docked.

"This is so exciting." Ellen was dressed for the occasion in jeans, white tennis shoes and a red pullover.

She carried a large navy tote bag and a small cooler. "It's been ages since we've been to the sea."

Rafe looked up to the clear blue sky and breathed in the salty tang on the light breeze. "It's a good day for it."

Flags fluttered from the sterns of sailboats moored on the other side of the marina. The waterway was lively with motorboats, skiffs and sailboats heading out for the day. Fishing boats were coming in with their catch, gulls wheeling around the rear of the vessels.

"Busy place," Darryl observed. A red baseball cap covered his sandy-colored hair and his windbreaker lay across his lap. "What do they charge you to moor here?"

"Too much," Rafe said. "I'm thinking of moving down the bay to someplace smaller."

He ushered them toward the makeshift ramp he'd improvised. Ellen began to assist Darryl in case his motorized wheelchair couldn't handle the steep incline.

"You go on ahead, Mum," Rafe said, taking over. "Drinks are in the cooler."

Ellen scurried up the ramp and onto the boat. "I brought some rolls and cold cuts and I made a banana loaf. I'll put them in the kitchen—that's the galley, right?"

Darryl sat upright in his chair, staring into the murky water rippling below the narrow ramp. "You've got life jackets, I presume? And an inflatable raft? What happens if we sink?"

"I've seen your arms, Dad. You could outswim an Olympic champion. Of course I've got life jackets and a raft." Rafe parked his father on the afterdeck. He took the beer bottle his mother handed him from the ice-filled cooler, twisted the cap off and gave it to his father. "Get one of these down your gullet. Relax and enjoy yourself."

"Ooh," Ellen said as she pulled a bottle of champagne out of the ice. "Is the sun over the yard-arm?"

"Help yourself. I know you like the bubbly." Rafe went inside the cabin and started the engines. At the sound, Colin, the silver-haired retiree whose yacht was moored in the neighboring berth, emerged from the cabin of his motor cruiser. He'd been standing by as prearranged, to cast them off. "Thanks, mate."

"No worries." Colin threw the lines on board as Rafe pulled away from the dock. "You can bring me a fresh fish if you have any spare."

Rafe motored slowly out of the marina and into open water. When they were a few miles from shore he put the engines in neutral and came down the gangway to the broad flat deck. His father was on his second beer, he noted with satisfaction. Good. Darryl deserved to enjoy himself.

He took a couple of fishing rods from the rack in

the corner of the deck and tried to hand one to his mother.

Ellen had found a cushioned seat in the sun. She shook her head, waving away his offer of the fishing rod. "I'm happy just to relax, thank you."

"What have you got for bait?" Darryl asked, inspecting the three-pronged hook.

Rafe heaved the lid off a built-in cooler and pulled out a bucket he had on ice. "Some squid I jigged off the pier last night."

He slid the bucket across the deck to his father. "We'll head down the bay and anchor off the point at Summerside. The snapper are biting there. That sound good?"

Darryl threaded a piece of cut-up squid onto his hook. "You really reckon you can make a business out of this?"

"I'll run fishing charters on the weekends." Rafe baited his hook and slotted the rod into the holder attached to the rail. "And supplement my income by doing income tax returns during the week. I've got a mini-office set up below in the master cabin. But my aim will be to gradually ease out of accounting to fish full-time."

"It sounds terrific," Ellen said.

Rafe made his voice deliberately casual as he asked, "What do you think, Dad?"

"I'll let you know if I catch a fish." Sitting up in his wheelchair, he drew his arm back and cast over

the side of the boat into the sparkling blue water.
Then he lifted his pale face to the sun, the rod held
loosely in his hands.

His dad had a habit of pretending to be grumpy
when he was most pleased. Rafe smiled and shook
his head. Today had given him an idea. He could alter
the boat to accommodate wheelchairs. There must
be more guys like his dad who would enjoy a day on
the bay with a rod and reel.

"I'll be up on the flying bridge if anyone wants
me." Rafe went up the gangway two steps at a time.
Behind the wheel, he put the boat in gear and motored slowly forward.

He heard footsteps and turned to see Ellen clinging to the rails, her wineglass clutched between her
fingers as she ascended.

"What a view!" She clinked her glass with his
soda can. "Congratulations, again."

He pulled out a folded chart from a pocket beneath
the instrument panel and pointed to a spot on the
coastline. "This is where we're going."

"Summerside Bay," Ellen read the name off the
chart. "Isn't that where you said Lexie lives?"

"Yeah." Rafe directed his gaze ahead, seeking out
the marker buoys.

"I don't want to pry but…"

"It's over between us." Rafe rounded the final buoy
marking the shipping channel and adjusted his course

to port. "We're back to where we started before she found out she was pregnant."

Ellen lifted her sunglasses to look at Rafe's face. "And where is that exactly?"

"Without the baby there's nothing to hold us together." He couldn't help the edge to his voice.

"Do you love her?"

He didn't speak for a moment. Then his mouth twisted. "It doesn't matter what I feel. She doesn't love me. She said so."

"Are you sure she really meant it?"

A speedboat went past loaded with young people, their laughter snatched away by the breeze. Rafe gripped the steering wheel as his boat bumped over their wake.

"Why wouldn't I believe her?" he asked, glancing at his mother. "Why would she lie about that?"

"Could be all sorts of reasons." Ellen sipped her champagne. "She's afraid of getting hurt. She's worried about the age difference. And don't forget, she's grieving for her baby. That will color how she feels about everything for a while."

The baby. He kept trying to put the pregnancy and miscarriage out of his mind but he couldn't stop wondering—had the baby been a boy or a girl? He wished he'd never seen the heartbeat on the sonogram.

"You sound as if you want me to get back together with her," he said.

"I want you to be happy," Ellen said, squeezing his

arm. She let a beat go by as a plane droned overhead. "Sometimes when people miscarry they have a small ceremony to honor the loss. Did she do anything like that?"

"I—I don't know." He glanced down at the compass and adjusted his course slightly. "I didn't think to ask."

He wished he hadn't been so cruel in some of the things he'd said.

"It's something to consider." Ellen patted his shoulder and went back down the gangway. "I'm going to see how your father's doing."

A moment later Rafe heard them speaking in low tones and laughing. After all the hardships they'd been through their love had stayed strong. He envied them their relationship.

Lexie had lost her baby.

And he had lost her.

Not that he'd ever had her.

LEXIE SAT on the couch with her legs up on the cushions, skirt spread out around her, staring out the window at the light gradually changing on the leaves of the gum trees. Two weeks had passed and she hadn't painted anything new since finishing Sienna's portrait. Instead she sat for hours at a time, blank and lost.

Rafe's parting words kept coming back to her. Was she punishing herself? Was that why she'd never married, never had children? The years had passed so fast. And she hadn't met the right guy.

There was no such thing as the "right" man.

In her heart there was only Rafe.

And he wasn't for her.

The doorbell rang. With an effort she roused herself and went to answer it.

She blinked. She'd been picturing Rafe in her mind. And there he was on her doorstep.

"I brought you something," he said. Two small stone statues were cradled in his arms. "Can I come in?"

She stepped back, her gaze riveted on the figurines. "What are those?"

Rafe slipped off his shoes and followed her into the living room. He set the statues on the dining table. Lexie came closer to study them. They were little children with round faces and long carved stone coats. Their hands were folded in front and their slanted eyes closed. Red crocheted caps sat on their heads and they wore little red bibs around their necks.

"They're mizuko kuyo—Japanese jizo statues," Rafe explained. "Mizuko kuyo literally means 'water children.' Jizo is the patron saint of women, children and travelers."

Lexie touched one smooth round stone cheek. "Where did you get them? What are they for?"

"I learned about them on the internet when I was looking up—"

She glanced up. His gaze was filled with compassion and something else…. Sadness?

"When I was looking up funeral ceremonies for miscarried babies," he finished quietly.

"Oh, Rafe." She touched his arm.

"Apparently the concept of mizuko is that existence flows slowly into a child and he or she gradually solidifies while growing in the womb." He took a breath, met her gaze. "Jizo helps miscarried, stillborn and aborted children find another pathway into being."

Tears filled her eyes. She couldn't speak.

"I thought we could have a ceremony. You could put them in your garden…." He trailed off.

"It's a beautiful idea. You brought two."

"I figured you probably never had any…closure," he said gruffly, as if uncomfortable with the term.

"Natalie said something about that the other day when I went for my checkup," Lexie said. "She told me the hospital holds ceremonies for miscarriages and stillbirths for parents who want it but I…I wasn't ready. This is better."

"I got a couple of pavers and stone pedestals from the garden center so they won't just sit on the grass," Rafe said. "I'll bring them through the carport to the back yard." Now that she'd accepted the statues he seemed anxious to get on and do something. "Have you got a wheelbarrow? The pedestals are heavy."

"In the carport. I'll go find a good spot." Lexie picked up one of the figurines. It was heavy and solid, about the size of a newborn. She carried it outside and looked around. Not near the trampoline. Or her studio...

She wandered to the far corner of the yard where the red camellia tree hung over the koi pond. In early spring the red petals drifted down onto the water. The corner was sheltered from the sun and the wind and from casual observation.

That's where her water babies would live.

"Over here," she called to Rafe.

He trundled the wheelbarrow over the bumpy ground. Lexie set the statue on the grass and went to get a shovel from the garden shed.

Rafe took it from her. "Do you want them side by side or on opposite sides of the pond?"

She studied the setting. "The tree is slightly off center. I think both of them on the left, next to each other." Her voice softened. "It seems cozier."

He started cutting into the turf, carefully digging out a rectangle. Lexie got her wicker basket and went through the gate in her fence to the path along the creek. There she collected wildflowers in purple, yellow and white.

By the time she returned, Rafe had positioned the paving squares at a slight angle to allow for the curving side of the pond.

"My brother Jack had a baby who died before he could be born, too," Lexie said. "His late wife was pregnant when she was killed in a plane crash." To herself, she added, "I should talk to him about that." To Rafe, she said, "What made you think of this?"

"My mother wondered if you'd had a ceremony." He lifted a chunk of dirt and grass and put it aside. "I wasn't sure."

He dusted the dirt from his hands. For a long moment their gazes held.

"You're welcome to visit the jizo statue anytime," Lexie said. She hesitated, not sure how far to push this. "It's your baby, too. Someday you might feel a need to…"

Rafe glanced away. He reached into the wheelbarrow and soon the only sound was the soft thunk of stone on concrete as he prepared the other pedestal. When he was done, he patch-worked small pieces of turf around the edges of the pavers to hide where the ground had been dug out.

Lexie went into the house for the other statue. They were almost exactly the same. She glanced at Rafe, who stepped back a respectful distance, and set the statue in place on the pedestal facing the pond. Her hands folded at her heart, she murmured a silent prayer for her first baby. *Forgive me, sweet one. Be at peace.*

Rafe picked up the other statue and held it out to her. She placed her hands over his on the stone figurine. "You do it."

He stood there so long, his dark eyes full of shadows, that she thought he was going to refuse. Then his mouth firmed and he accepted it from her. He placed it on the pedestal, taking a long time to make sure it was centered.

Then he stepped back and turned to her. She walked into his embrace and his arms folded around her, warm and solid and strong. They stood together with just the sound of the birds and the faint rattle of the gum leaves in the breeze. A long slender leaf fell and landed on the edge of one of the pedestals, making the two stone children look as if they'd been there for a long time.

"I—I'm sorry, Lexie." His low voice broke. "Sorry I said I was relieved. I was wrong to say that. I didn't know— You were right. I need to grow up."

"Shh, it's okay."

It was late afternoon, the hour when everything was burnished with a golden light. Rafe stood by while Lexie spread the delicate flowers at the base of the statues. When it was done she whispered another quiet prayer. And turned to Rafe. "Thank you. I will never forget this. Or you."

"Lexie." He took her in his arms again and kissed

her. Tender, healing kisses pressed over her wet eyes and soft mouth. Lexie clung to him.

"Lexie," he murmured. "We could try again."

She longed to. But after today and seeing the tenderness he was capable of, she just couldn't.

"Rafe," she said, agonized. "You might not think you want children but that could change in the future. Y-you deserve a younger woman, one who can give you healthy babies—"

"But I don't—" He broke off. She read his doubt.

"You see? Even you don't know what you'll want in the future. Five years from now you might like to have a family. By then I'll be too old."

"But I would have you."

"I'm not going to take options away from you," she said around a lump in her throat. "Anyway, I—I don't love you. Remember?"

RAFE KNOCKED on Hetty's door. Lexie's rejection following the mizuko ceremony had wounded him more than he'd expected.

He almost didn't recognize the woman who opened the door. Hetty was wearing a pair of jeans and a multicolored blouse. This was the first time he'd seen her without her trademark tunic and flowing pants.

He handed her a bag containing a couple of snapper. "Thought you might like some fresh fish."

"Why, thank you." Hetty stepped back. "Come in.

Steve's over at Jack's workshop but he shouldn't be long."

"It's you I wanted to talk to." Rafe felt foolish but he figured he might as well just come out with it. "I need some advice. About Lexie."

"I'll make a pot of tea. Come through to the kitchen." Hetty led the way to a sunny room overlooking the backyard. A basket of washing waited by the door to be hung out on the clothesline.

"I'd prefer coffee, if it's not too much trouble," Rafe said, taking a seat at the breakfast table.

"One coffee, coming right up." She bustled around, filling the kettle, spooning ground coffee into a plunger.

"You're looking well," he said. "Your hair's different, longer. It's nice."

"Thanks." She touched her silvery-gray hair that now had a slight curl at the ends. "I got tired of the spiky look."

Rafe sipped his coffee. "How are you and Steve?"

"We're getting there," Hetty said. "I'm going to Toastmasters and Steve is trying yoga. Lexie's idea. She insisted. I don't know if it'll work but we're making the effort, at least."

She picked up the laundry basket. "Would you mind coming outside while I hang this up? I want to get it dry before dark."

"Sure. I'll give you a hand." He followed past some garden furniture arranged on the deck and down the steps to a narrow concrete path to the rotary clothes-line in the middle of the yard. On the sunny side of the yard was a vegetable patch, the summer crop over and the earth turned for autumn planting.

Hetty put the basket on the ground and bent to pick up a handful of socks. "Lexie told me about the jizo statues. That was a lovely gesture. It meant so much to her."

Rafe sipped his coffee and handed her clothes pegs from the bucket attached to the central post. "She pushed me away afterward, saying that I should find a younger woman. I used to be certain I didn't want kids. I still don't feel ready but maybe someday…"

"Timing is important in life. To marry, to have children." Hetty pinned up one of Steve's plaid shirts. "Lexie is running out of time. If you want to be with her, you'd have to make a decision soon and stick with it."

"I'd do just about anything to make her happy. I'd like us to at least have the chance to know each other better. To see if we could be a couple."

Hetty grabbed a pair of trousers from the basket and shook them out. "She said you asked her to marry you and she said no."

"She told me she didn't love me. I guess I should just get it through my head that she doesn't want me but—"

"But what?"

Rafe watched a magpie pull up a worm from the grass. "I don't believe her."

"Be patient with her. She's still grieving." Hetty pinned the trousers to the line, then paused. "Do *you* love *her?*"

"That's what I want to find out," Rafe said. "I can't do it unless we spend time together."

Hetty bent for another shirt and smiled at him. "Remember the advice you gave me? Don't give up and don't go away."

"You want me to stalk her?" he asked doubtfully.

"No!" She swung the clothesline around to a free space. "Obviously I don't mean for you to do anything creepy. Prove that you want to be with her by simply being available. Be a friend to her. Don't get scared and run off. A wise young man once told me that it takes time to build trust."

"I would need to be nearby," Rafe said, his mind ticking over the possibilities. "I was already planning to move my boat farther down the bay."

"Mornington has a nice marina," Hetty commented. "And it isn't far from Summerside."

"That's true." He drained his coffee, eager to put a new plan into action. "I'd better get going. Thanks."

Hetty left the laundry and walked him to the door. "Good luck. I hope we see you again soon."

"I hope so, too." Rafe paused on the doorstep. "What would a guy wear to yoga class?"

Hetty smiled. "Steve just wears a T-shirt and shorts."

CHAPTER FIFTEEN

RAFE STOOD outside Lexie's front door, Murphy at his feet. He probably should have called before coming over but it would be harder for her to tell him to go away in person.

"I'm not asking for a lot," he said to Murphy. "Just a bit of her time." The dog tilted his head and whined.

Rafe took a deep breath and knocked.

Lexie opened the door wearing jeans and a blue T-shirt that brought out the color of her eyes. "Rafe!"

"You said once you'd teach me yoga." He held up his brand-new rolled-up mat.

"*Now?* I—I would but…" She glanced down at his gray shorts and bare feet in flip-flops. Then over his shoulder at the road. "Sally's dropping Chloe off for me to babysit any minute."

"Oh."

"Come in. We can do a couple moves before they get here." She glanced over her shoulder. "It *is* just yoga."

"Yes." He drank in her eyes, her mouth, her perfume.

For now.

"Okay, well…" She glanced around, clearly flustered. "You move the furniture out of the way while I go get changed." She went off down the hall.

Rafe pushed the coffee table against the couch and pulled the chintz-covered armchair to the opposite wall. He unrolled his yoga mat. Murphy came over to inspect it and he nudged him away. "This isn't for you, buddy. Go lie down."

Lexie came back in a clinging tank top and stretchy close-fitting pants. She blushed as he took her in.

She unrolled her mat a few feet away from his. "We'll start with Sun Salutation. Hands together in front."

Feeling foolish, Rafe followed her lead and pressed his palms as if in prayer.

"Breathe in and raise your arms above your head," Lexie instructed. "On the exhale fold forward, chest resting on thighs, hands on the floor."

Hands on the floor? Was she kidding? Rafe's knuckles dangled just below his knees. Clearly his weekly basketball games weren't doing much for his flexibility.

"Now bring your right leg back in a lunge, chest up, hips down," Lexie went on. "No, hips *down*."

"They are down," Rafe grunted over the sound of his left knee cracking.

Lexie got up and came around to his side. Her small hands gripped his hips and gently pressed.

He felt a tightening of his groin from her touch....

"Don't stiffen up," she said. "Ease into it. Chest up." Now her hands were on his shoulders, pulling them back. Her long hair brushed his bare arms and he breathed in her scent. It was torture to be so near her.

"Now put your left leg back beside your right, and bring your body forward over your hands, keeping straight and rigid like a plank."

Finally, something he could do. This was like a pushup.

Lexie moved in front of him and got down on the floor in the same position but facing him. Allowing him a clear view of her cleavage.

"Lower yourself to the ground slowly," she said. "Touching down with your chin, chest, knees."

"This doesn't feel relaxing," Rafe muttered.

"Now lay your whole body down. Lift your head and arch your back, looking up at the ceiling. This is Cobra pose. Great for those knotted neck and back muscles." He'd just gotten used to that when she said, "Now to Downward Dog. Up on your hands and feet. Push your butt high in the air, legs and arms straight in an A shape."

Rafe peered through his hair to figure out what she meant. Her tight round butt encased in blue spandex was outlined against the cream-colored wall. Her blond hair hung between her arms.

He hoisted himself into the position. And a pretty undignified position it was, too.

The doorbell rang.

"That'll be Sally. I'll just be a second." Lexie bounced to her feet. "Stay in Downward Dog. It's a fantastic hamstring stretch."

Stay. Stay, boy. But he had to admit, the stretch did feel good.

Then Murphy trotted over and started licking his face with big slurps. "Stop it, Murph. Good dog. Go away. Murph!"

"Hey, Andrew!" Lexie exclaimed. "Come in."

Uh-oh. Who the heck was Andrew?

Between his legs he saw Lexie's shapely ankles and bare feet return to the living room followed by…a small pair of running shoes with the laces undone. Rafe tilted his head and his gaze shifted upward to a pair of skinny legs and two scabby knees.

Andrew was a little boy.

Rafe started to unfold.

"Don't move," Lexie cried. "You need to finish the sequence." She made him lunge his right leg forward then bring his left in before rising and lifting

his arms above his head again. Then he had to pull
them together at his *heart center*.

And all the while he was being stared at by a pair
of unblinking hazel eyes in a freckly face. It was
unnerving.

"Namaste," Lexie said.

"Why is he in his underwear?" Andrew asked
with a lisp.

"These are shorts, kid," Rafe said. Anyone could
tell the difference.

"They look like my dad's underwear."

Lexie crouched to tie the boy's shoelaces. "We
were doing yoga. You've seen me doing yoga before.
This is Rafe. Rafe, this is Andrew who lives next
door."

"Can I get my ball?" Andrew said, reaching for
Lexie's hand. "It went over the fence."

"Of course you can. Come with me." Lexie led
him out through the kitchen. She glanced over her
shoulder at Rafe. "I'll be right back."

"Sure." It was all he could do not to follow.
Murphy, the traitor, trotted after Lexie and Andrew,
tail wagging.

The doorbell rang again.

Rafe glanced out the window. Lexie and Andrew
were searching the hydrangea bushes for his ball. He
went to answer the door.

Sally stood there with Chloe on her hip. Her brown

hair was pulled into a disheveled ponytail. "Rafe, isn't it? Lexie's expecting me."

"She's outside with the boy from next door. Come on in." He stepped back. "I'll call her."

"Oh, don't bother." Sally glanced at her watch. "I'm already late. If it's okay with you, I'll just get Chloe set up and take off." She spread a blanket on the floor and plunked the curly-headed tot in the middle of it. "Wait a minute. You're the one from the barbecue."'

Rafe raised his hands. "I swear I won't touch a hair on her head. Your baby will be safe."

"Okay." She upended a tote bag of toys. "Tell Lexie I'll talk to her when I get back from my doctor's appointment. Bye-bye, pumpkin." She blew kisses to Chloe. "I'll be back very soon." And then she was running out the door.

Chloe looked at the door closing behind her mother. Her bottom lip wobbled. She grabbed a toy and tossed it down again. Then she raised her arms to Rafe. "Up."

"You don't like me, remember?" Rafe said, without moving.

She stretched her arms so enthusiastically her pink corduroy butt lifted off the ground. *"Up."*

Rafe went to the window. He tapped on it and mimed rocking a baby. Lexie nodded and held up a finger. She and Andrew were still combing the bushes for the ball.

Rafe pushed a brightly colored plastic toy toward Chloe with his toe. "Here, play with this."

She ignored it and continued to reach for him and grunt.

"Oh all right." Rafe bent to pick her up. She was heavier than the last time he'd held her.

At least she wasn't crying this time. Her hazel eyes were enormous. Her hair had grown, too, into soft curls that framed her round face.

Chloe poked him in the cheek and gurgled, showing off four tiny bottom teeth. Then she pulled off a bootie and dropped it.

"You lost your bootie," Rafe said sarcastically.

She pointed at it and grunted.

"For crying out loud." He bent at the knees, trying to keep Chloe upright, and laboriously retrieved the limp piece of knitting. He'd no sooner straightened and was trying to jam it back on her chubby foot than Chloe giggled and pulled off her other bootie. With a gleeful smile she held it out, her eyes on his, and dropped it deliberately.

The little minx.

"It would serve you right if I left that there for the dog to chew. Murphy, where are you?" He glanced around, pretending to look for the dog.

Lexie was in the doorway, watching him with a

smile on her face. "Andrew's throwing his ball for Murphy." She nodded at Chloe. "She likes you."

"She's a master at manipulation." He walked over to Lexie and tried to hand Chloe over. The girl knotted her tiny fists in his shirt and clung.

"Quit jerking my chain." Rafe gave Chloe a look, letting her know he was onto her. Gently, he pried her fingers loose from the fabric. She immediately curled them around his thumb, looking up at him with those big eyes. Something funny happened to his stomach. And it wasn't a twinge of pain. "Here, take her."

"Look at the silly man," Lexie crooned in a baby voice to Chloe. "Rafe's afraid of a little girl."

Damn right he was. "Uh, maybe I'd better get going. You're busy with the kids."

"You can stay if you want."

"Nah." He rolled his mat. "I've got things to do on the boat." He met her gaze. "Another time?"

"Sure." She walked him to the door. "Mum said you were thinking of moving your boat to Mornington."

"I'm there now. Come down and visit. Anytime."

Looking thoughtful, Lexie swayed Chloe in her arms then slowly closed the door.

LEXIE PARKED her car at the marina, grabbed her box of paints from the trunk and walked across to the pier. Gulls circled the back of the seafood restaurant on stilts over the water. The stays on the sailboats in the harbor clanked gently. She walked down the long concrete pier, grateful for her sweater. The unseasonably warm days had passed and autumn had arrived.

When she saw Rafe's sandwich board advertising his fishing charter rates, her heart beat faster. The boat was tied up broadside to the pier. Rafe was on the back deck, hosing out the big coolers. He was wearing a navy pullover and gumboots over his jeans. His thick black hair moved in the breeze.

Murphy poked his furry head out of the cabin and barked once then scampered across the wet deck, tail wagging.

"Quiet, Murph," Rafe said without looking up.

"Ahoy there, matie!" Lexie called, clutching the handle of her wooden box.

Rafe straightened abruptly. He dropped the hose and jumped onto the pier to turn off the tap. Wiping his hands on the back of his jeans, he nodded at the boat. "What do you think?"

"Awesome." Lexie lifted her box. "I came to paint the name on it for you. I take it—" she glanced at the existing name in flowing script across the bow "—*Mikonos Princess,* is the previous owner's name for the boat. Have you got a new name?"

He stood beside her to study the forty-seven-foot craft. "I was going to call it *Someday*."

"That doesn't apply anymore, does it?" she asked.

Rafe's gaze flicked to her before he turned back to the boat. "Lately I've been thinking of naming it *Yin Yang*."

"I like it," she said. *Was that a reference to her?* "I could paint the symbol after the name."

"While I was researching mizuko kuyo I looked up the term," he said casually. "Yin and Yang *are* opposites but they're also—"

"Two sides to the same coin," she finished.

"Two halves that make up a whole." He turned to her, his gaze searching. "What do you think? Are we two halves of a whole?"

Lexie swallowed. For a long moment, she stared at him. *Were* they two halves of a whole? Could she really have found her soul mate in this unlikely man?

"You left in a hurry earlier," she said.

Rafe glanced down at his gumboots and scuffed the pier. "Hetty said I should be patient with you. Thing is, you'd need to be patient with me, too."

"Rafe! Hey, mate, howya doing?" a man called from about thirty feet away. "You ready to rock and roll?"

Lexie glanced over to see a tall blond man with

glasses and a petite brunette approaching. They carried a cooler between them. The man had a baby backpack strapped on. A little blond boy about a year old peered around his dad's shoulder.

Everyone seemed to have babies, Lexie thought with a sudden stab of pain. Except for her.

"Hey, Chris, Laura." Rafe looked back to Lexie. "I used to work with Chris. I'm taking them out fishing. Do you want to come?"

"I...have things I need to do." She took a step back. Being with Chloe was one thing; she'd known her for so long. But she wasn't ready to coo over a stranger's baby. "I've realized my little box of paints isn't going to do the trick. I'm going to need marine enamel. And heavy duty solvent to strip the old paint."

"I'll take off the old paint." Rafe glanced sideways at his approaching friends. Then he met Lexie's gaze straight on. "I don't believe you when you say you don't love me."

"Rafe—"

"Shh, they're almost here and I want to say this." He spoke more urgently. "I don't know what the future holds. I only know that I want to be with you. You and me. Everything else is negotiable."

And then his friends were there, exclaiming over the boat. Eyeing her curiously.

She smiled at the couple then spun and walked

away. It was too late to tell herself she wasn't going to get involved with a younger man.

She loved him.

The realization made her stop dead in the middle of the wharf. This was about so much more than just sex, or friendship, or whether or not to have a child. This was about the rest of her life.

She started walking again, faster. Her heart was well and truly on the line.

And despite herself, her fisherman was slowly reeling her in.

LEXIE SHUT OFF the water and stepped out of the shower. She was reaching for a towel when the doorbell rang. She dried herself hastily, wondering who could be calling at nine in the evening. She threw on a pale blue silk dressing gown and hurried barefoot down the hall.

Ding Dong.

"Hold your horses," she called, and opened the door.

"Hey, Lexie." Rafe stood on her doorstep.

"Rafe!" She pressed a hand to her heart. "What are you doing here? I thought you would have spent the evening with your friends."

"All that fresh air exhausted them." He presented her with a bucket. "I brought you some fish. Fancy a late dinner?"

"Thanks." She peered at two beautiful snapper, cleaned and scaled, nestled on ice. Then she looked back at Rafe, sexier than a man had any right to be in a jacket over a white T-shirt and jeans. His hair was slightly damp. He must have showered, too, before he came over.

"I've already eaten but I can always put away some fresh fish."

"Is my first mate welcome, too?"

Lexie laughed. "Why not?"

Rafe glanced over his shoulder and whistled. Murphy poked his head out of the open window of the Mazda. He didn't need any further invitation to leap through and bound up the path to the front door.

She stepped back, suddenly aware that the thin silk of her dressing gown was sticking to her. "Take these to the kitchen," she said, handing the bucket back to him. "I'll go get dressed."

Then she fled down the hall to her bedroom. What to wear? Jeans, a skirt…sexy lingerie? She pulled open a drawer and started dragging clothes out and throwing them on her bed.

"Lexie?" Rafe stood outside her open doorway. He'd taken his jacket off and his arms were tanned and strong below the sleeves of his T-shirt. "What did you do with the frying pan?"

"It's in the fridge, full of leftover fried rice. I was caught up in painting. I'll clean it out in a minute."

"Take your time." He started to leave.

Lexie reached for the garment on the top of the pile. It was a wraparound skirt. She heard footsteps returning and fumbled with the tie, trying to loosen it from its slot—

And then Rafe was right there, wrapping his arms around her, burying his face in her hair, enveloping her with his scent and his heat and his strength. "I *love* you."

He loved her.

Emotion welled up in her, choking her.

"I should have said it before," he went on. "I love you. Please don't send me away again."

She turned in his arms and pressed her face against his chest. She could hear his heart racing. Then he was pushing back her hair, lifting her chin, seeking her lips with his own.

She twined herself around him, kissing his neck, his stubbled jaw.

"It doesn't matter if you don't love me right away," he said. "Just give me a chance. I'll prove I'm not going anywhere."

"Rafe." She could hardly speak for the lump in her throat. "I don't want you to go anywhere."

He took her mouth in a long deep kiss, running his hands over her shoulders and down her back. "I've missed you. You don't know how hard it's been to keep away."

She eased back to look at him. "I almost called you so many times."

Rafe released her and swept the clothes off her bed. He glanced around and then dumped them on top of her dresser. Then he sat on the bed and opened his arms. "Come here."

Lexie went to him. He laid her down and kissed her. His hand slipped inside her dressing gown to cup her breast. She pushed her fingers through his hair, marveling at how silky it felt. She moved her mouth over his lips, his jaw and down his neck, taking in his male heat and the salty taste of his skin.

She let her gown slip open, an invitation to touch her.

But in spite of the hard ridge inside his jeans he seemed content to kiss and fondle her above the waist. His callused thumb rasped over her nipple and she moaned softly. Impatient, she eased back and started to undo the stud on his jeans.

His hand stilled hers. "Are you sure it's okay? I mean, you weren't hurt inside from losing the baby?"

"My doctor gave me the all clear."

He kissed her again. "But we'll take it slow."

Her smile spread. "I like it slow."

Rafe shucked his jeans and pulled his T-shirt over

his head. Lying on his side, he parted her dressing gown and stroked one full breast then dipped to her belly.

Lexie brushed the hair off his forehead. He lifted his gaze and found her watching him. A rush of warmth welled in him that he couldn't have imagined feeling a few short months ago.

He slid up and kissed her again, kissed her tears away. Gradually the tenor of their caresses changed. She shifted beneath him, opening her arms, opening herself. The blue of her eyes deepened.

Rafe leaned over the side of the bed and pulled a condom out of his jeans pocket. "If you get pregnant again it's going to be because we planned it."

Lexie took it from him and ripped the package open. She sheathed him, rolling the condom on so slowly he thought he was going to lose his mind. The need to be inside her became overwhelming.

Rafe rocked forward, pushing into her, his body taut. She wrapped her legs around his hips, urging him deeper. He tried to hold back but she was moving faster now, her breath coming in pants. His need built with each thrust. Lexie's eyes, scant inches away, were all he saw. Then her body arched and her head fell back, eyes closing. Feeling her dissolve beneath him, Rafe let go....

LEXIE AWOKE the next morning to the phone ringing. Sleepily she raised her head to look at the clock.

Ten o'clock. Rafe murmured in his sleep and his arm around her tightened. His thick dark hair was tousled and the tangled sheets had slipped to his hips.

Lexie eased herself out of bed regretfully and ran lightly down the hall. She followed the sound of her cell phone to the dining table and found it next to a stack of old mail.

"Hello?" she said.

"This is Andrea McCall from the Archibald Prize Foundation at the Art Gallery of New South Wales," a woman said. "May I speak with Ms. Lexie Thatcher?"

Lexie's mouth dried. Her heart racing, she said, "This is she."

"Lexie," Andrea went on less formally. "I'm very pleased to tell you that your painting, *Sienna,* has been chosen as a finalist."

"Oh, my God! I can't believe it," Lexie squealed, dancing on the spot. "Thank you!"

"You'll receive an official notice in the mail," Andrea went on. "Plus an invitation to the awards luncheon."

"Can I bring a guest?" Lexie asked.

"You may fill one table with guests. Each table seats ten."

"Fantastic!" Lexie said. "My whole family can come."

Andrea bade her goodbye to continue making her

calls. Lexie hung up feeling as if she was walking on air. She picked up a sleeping Yin and twirled around, making the cat's eyes widen with alarm. "I did it! I'm a finalist!"

She set Yin down and ran back to her bedroom. Rafe was groggily opening his eyes and stretching.

"Get up!" She pounced on him. "My portrait of Sienna finaled in the Archibald! We're going to Sydney."

Rafe rubbed his eyes. "Now?"

"In two weeks." She grinned like an idiot.

"In that case," he said, pulling her into his arms. "We've got time for a cuddle."

"DID YOU BRING your blue dress that matches the robe in the painting?" Lexie said to Sienna, waving her glass of champagne. "You have to wear the blue dress."

The whole family—Hetty and Steve; Jack, Sienna and Oliver; Renita, Brett and Tegan; Lexie and Rafe—had booked a four-bedroom suite in the Sofitel Hotel in Sydney where the awards luncheon was being held. They'd arrived en masse in taxis from the airport and immediately called room service to order champagne.

"I'll wear the blue dress, even though no one will be looking at me. You're the star." Sienna glanced around at the assembled family and raised her glass of champagne. "To Lexie!"

"To Lexie! To winning the prize! Hear, hear!" came a chorus of murmured toasts.

Lexie grinned and sipped her drink although she didn't need champagne to give her a bubbly feeling. Thank goodness Rafe's arm was wrapped firmly around her waist or she might have floated away. She glanced up at him, aglow with excitement. His return smile warmed her.

"We'd better get ready." Renita put down her glass and got up from the couch. She gave her sister a hug. "I'm so excited for you."

Brett touched Lexie's shoulder as he passed. "You're going to win."

Lexie put her hands over her ears. "Don't jinx me."

Everyone went back to their rooms to get ready for the luncheon. Lexie had bought a new dress for the occasion, pale blue linen over which she cinched a stretchy belt with a huge silver buckle. Her long hair she left loose, a tangle of blond curls around her shoulders.

"Everyone expects me to win," she said to Rafe, slipping long dangly silver earrings into her ears. "What if I don't?"

"I don't expect you to win," Rafe said, putting on his jacket. When Lexie's eyebrows rose, he explained, "There are thirty-four finalists. The odds are terrible."

"You're right." Lexie stepped into her high heels. "In some strange way, that makes me feel better."

"Don't get me wrong," Rafe said, cupping her face to kiss her. "I think your painting is amazing. And I hope you win for your sake. But if you don't, you'll still be a terrific artist."

"Thank you." Lexie stretched up and kissed him. "But you have to admit, the money would come in handy."

Rafe hesitated, his hand on the doorknob. "I wasn't going to tell you this yet but…Larry called yesterday. He offered me my job back."

Lexie rocked back on her heels to search his face. "What did you say?"

"I told him I'd have to think about it." His mouth twisted. "As you say, we could use the money."

"Don't do it," Lexie said fiercely. "You love the boat. You've had two fishing charters already. And there's your freelance accounting."

"Those two charters taught me how much I have to learn about this business. I got the wrong bait. Some of the guys weren't happy. Besides, the money I've earned so far won't pay the bills." He shrugged. "Larry's offer is something to consider."

Lexie thought about it as they rode down in the elevator. What Rafe hadn't said was, they were a unit now. He wanted to be able to provide for her, as well, when her paintings weren't selling. She'd paid the first installment on her taxes but there was another due next week. Rafe was trying to take the pressure off her by saying he didn't care if she won or not.

But *she* cared. She wanted that $50,000 prize money. It would be enough to pay her taxes and penalties and tide Rafe over until he got his business on its feet. So he wouldn't ever have to go back to the tax office.

The ballroom at the hotel was rapidly filling with finalists and guests as Lexie and her entourage made their way across the carpeted lobby. They showed their tickets at the door and were directed to their table up front.

Lexie tried to enjoy lunch, to savor the moment. Between courses she met Andrea McCall, the judging panelists, and chatted with some of her fellow finalists. The speeches seemed to go on forever. All she could think about was what winning would mean to her and Rafe.

On the stage, Andrea tapped the microphone. "The time has come, ladies and gentlemen, to give out the award for the Archibald Prize. The finalists are..." And she read out the long list of names.

Lexie's spirits sank. She'd known there were lots but to hear them all...

Beneath the table, Rafe took her hand and murmured into her ear, "And the winner is...Lexie Thatcher."

"Stop that," she said, laughing nervously. "Not funny."

"And now for the award. We only announce the winner and the runner up. In second place is…" Andrea opened an envelope, scanned the contents and spoke into the microphone. "Alexander Greene."

A round of applause broke out over the ballroom. Alexander Greene, a bearded man in his sixties wearing a dinner jacket over jeans up went to receive his plaque.

When he'd returned to his seat, Andrea said, "And now, for first prize…."

Lexie's grip tightened on Rafe's hand. She glanced around the table. Jack gave her a thumbs-up. Hetty smiled encouragement. Renita, sitting next to her, gave her a hug. Steve was facing the stage but he glanced over his shoulder and nodded. Brett, Sienna, Oliver and Tegan all glanced her way before turning at the sound of the envelope being opened.

She exchanged a quick glance with Rafe. He smiled nervously. She held her breath.

"The winner is…"

Lexie Thatcher. Lexie Thatcher. Lexie Thatcher.

"Julianne Mayer!"

Lexie was enclosed in a bubble, surrounded by the roar of applause, separated from every other person by a transparent sphere of disappointment. Dimly she was aware of herself clapping for the winner. Smiling and shrugging at her sympathetic family. "It's fine. I'm good. It doesn't matter. Being a finalist is reward enough."

Part of her truly believed that. Part of her believed that simply having painted the best work of her career to date more than compensated for not winning. She didn't care about the accolades or the money for its own sake. She'd long ago accepted that borderline poverty was the price she paid for doing what she did.

But still. It would have been nice to win.

"Don't call Larry," she said, putting her hand on Rafe's arm. "We'll get by, somehow."

LEXIE HAD just closed the front door behind her when the phone began to ring inside the house.

"Leave it," Rafe said. "We'll miss the sunset."

A week had passed since the Archibald Prize luncheon. Rafe was doing everything he could to make it up to her for the disappointments she'd had—first the baby, then losing the prize. This evening they were going out on the boat for a romantic cruise, just the two of them. And of course, Murphy, the first mate.

The phone continued to ring.

Lexie hesitated, looked over her shoulder. "I feel strange. Kind of prickly all over. I want to answer that."

"Get it then," Rafe said. "Murphy and I will be in the car."

She went back inside.

Rafe held the back door open and whistled. Murphy hopped in. Rafe got into the driver's seat and rolled down the window. He was tuning the radio to a classical station when Lexie stepped onto the porch.

With her graceful figure in cotton fisherman pants and a fitted top, she was quite a picture. The thought flashed through him, *I am a lucky man*.

"Rafe. Guess what?" She was grinning like a fool.

"What?" he asked, laughing.

"That was Samuel. The National Gallery of Victoria wants to buy my portrait of Sienna."

"That's good." He turned the key in the ignition.

"Good? You don't understand. It's fantastic." She got into the car and threw her arms around his neck. "It's better than the Archibald Prize. Sixty-five thousand dollars!"

"Not bad for a few months' work." He was teasing her, making her think he didn't understand what a huge deal this was. "Does this mean we'll be able to afford chicken with our two-minute noodles?"

"Hell, we'll be able to eat filet mignon." She went quiet as she fastened her seat belt. Then she glanced at him. "Maybe we'll stick to rump steak for a while."

He gave up the pretense and hugged her enthusiastically. "Rump steak, chicken—who cares? Congratulations, Lexie! I always knew you were the best. And now the whole country will, too."

Rafe backed out of the driveway and set off down the quiet residential street toward the glassy bay where the setting sun was already turning the water to molten gold.

He reached for Lexie's hand and felt her fingers squeeze his. Some people might say the odds were against them as a couple….

But he thought they just might be on a winning streak.

* * * * *

COMING NEXT MONTH

Available April 12, 2011

#1698 RETURN TO THE BLACK HILLS
Spotlight on Sentinel Pass
Debra Salonen

#1699 THEN THERE WERE THREE
Count on a Cop
Jeanie London

#1700 A CHANCE IN THE NIGHT
Mama Jo's Boys
Kimberly Van Meter

#1701 A SCORE TO SETTLE
Project Justice
Kara Lennox

#1702 BURNING AMBITION
The Texas Firefighters
Amy Knupp

#1703 DESERVING OF LUKE
Going Back
Tracy Wolff

You can find more information on upcoming
Harlequin® titles, free excerpts and more at
www.HarlequinInsideRomance.com.

HSRCNM0311

Selene wanted nothing to do with the father of her son, Alex; but Aristedes had other plans...that included them.

Read on for an sneak peek from
THE SARANTOS SECRET BABY by Olivia Gates,
available April 2011, only from Harlequin Desire.

"You were right to turn my marriage offer down," Aristedes said.

And Selene found her voice at last, found the words that would not betray the blow he'd dealt her. "Thanks for letting me know. You didn't have to come all the way here, though. You could have just let it go. I left yesterday with the understanding that this case is closed."

Before the hot needles behind her eyes could dissolve into an unforgivable display of stupidity and weakness, she began to close the door.

The door stopped against an immovable object. His flat palm.

"I can't accept that." His voice was low, leashed.

What did her tormentor mean now? Was he ending one game only to start another?

She raised eyes as bruised as her self-respect to his, found nothing there but solemnity and determination.

Before she could voice her confusion, he elaborated. "I never let anything go unless I'm certain it's unworkable. I realize I made you an unworkable offer, and that's why I'm withdrawing it. I'm here to offer something else. A workability study."

She leaned against the door, thankful for its support and partial shield. "Your son and I are not a business venture you can test for feasibility."

His gaze grew deeper, made her feel as if he was trying to delve into her mind, take control of it. "It's actually the other way around. I'm the one who would be tested."

She shook her head. "Why bother? I know—and *you* know—you're not workable. Not with me."

His spectacular eyebrows lowered over eyes she felt were emitting silver hypnosis. "You're right again. Neither you nor I have any reason to believe that isn't the truth. The only truth. It might be best for both you and Alex to never hear from me again, to forget I exist. But then again, maybe not. I'm only asking for the chance for both of us to find out for certain. You believe I'm unworkable in any personal relationship. I've lived my life based on that belief about myself. I never really had reason to question it. But I have one now. In fact, I have two."

Find out what happens in
THE SARANTOS SECRET BABY by Olivia Gates,
available April 2011, only from Harlequin Desire.

SPECIAL EDITION

Life, Love, Family and Top Authors!

In April, Harlequin Special Edition features
four *USA TODAY* bestselling authors!

FORTUNE'S JUST DESSERTS
by MARIE FERRARELLA

Follow the latest drama featuring the ever-powerful
and passionate Fortune family.

YOURS, MINE & OURS
by JENNIFER GREEN

Life can't get any more chaotic for Amanda Scott.
Divorced and a single mom, Amanda had given up on
the knight-in-shining-armor fairy tale until a friendship
with Mike becomes something a little more....

THE BRIDE PLAN (*SECOND-CHANCE BRIDAL* MINISERIES)
by KASEY MICHAELS

Finding love and second chances for others is
second nature for bridal-shop owner Chessie.
But will *she* finally get her second chance?

THE RANCHER'S DANCE
by ALLISON LEIGH

Return to the Double C Ranch this month—where love, loss
and new beginnings set the stage for Allison Leigh's latest title.

*Look for these titles and others in April 2011
from Harlequin Special Edition, wherever books are sold.*

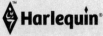

♥ Harlequin®

A *Romance* FOR EVERY MOOD™

www.eHarlequin.com

SEUSA0411

Harlequin® Romance

MARGARET WAY

In the Australian Billionaire's Arms

Handsome billionaire David Wainwright isn't about to let his favorite uncle be taken for all he's worth by mysterious and undeniably attractive florist Sonya Erickson.

But David soon discovers that Sonya's no greedy gold digger. And as sparks sizzle between them, will the rugged Australian embrace the secrets of her past so they can have a chance at a future together?

Don't miss this incredible new tale, available in April 2011 wherever books are sold!

Harlequin®

A *Romance* FOR EVERY MOOD™

www.eHarlequin.com

HR17722

Love Inspired®

Top authors

Janet Tronstad and Debra Clopton

bring readers two heartwarming stories,
where estranged sisters find family and love in
this very special collection celebrating motherhood!

Available April 2011.

www.SteepleHill.com

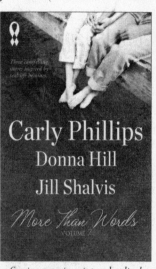